Frederick A. Ober

Rambles in Sunny Spain

Frederick A. Ober

Rambles in Sunny Spain

ISBN/EAN: 9783337239886

Printed in Europe, USA, Canada, Australia, Japan

Cover: Foto ©Andreas Hilbeck / pixelio.de

More available books at **www.hansebooks.com**

PASS OF THE DESPENAPEROS, BETWEEN GRANADA AND BARCELONA.

RAMBLES

IN

SUNNY SPAIN.

By FRED A. OBER.

FULLY ILLUSTRATED.

BOSTON
ESTES AND LAURIAT
PUBLISHERS

CONTENTS.

ILLUSTRATIONS.

RAMBLES IN SUNNY SPAIN.

Rambles in Sunny Spain.

HEN one has the world to choose from, but only a limited time for travel, he is apt to look about sharply for a country that will yield the most in return for his outlay.

This was the feeling that actuated us in the choice of Spain. We felt that we should get greater returns for our summer's journey than from any other equal portion of the globe. In the first place, our little travels hitherto taken had in a measure prepared us for Spain. In Florida we had met with Spanish architecture (especially in St. Augustine) and Spanish names of rivers, lakes, and towns, while the most fascinating portion of Florida's history is that which tells of the adventures of the steel-clad cavaliers of De Soto and De Narvaez. If in the land of the Everglades we had been led to think upon Spain as the "mother-country," in the West Indies again everything still pointed back to that land of the olive and the vine, that home of Ponce de Leon, Cortez, and Columbus.

So it was, gentle reader, that our thoughts gradually shaped themselves; and by the time we were prepared for another journey, we had settled upon Spain as the object of it. Without mentioning any other reason than that its historical associations fascinated us, is not this alone enough to account for our choice? No other land of

A SPANISH COURTYARD.

the Eastern Hemisphere is so intimately connected with the early history of America. And in view of the near approach of the four hundredth anniversary of the first voyage of Columbus (in 1492), we believe that there will be a revival of interest in all things pertaining to early Spain. Thus we reasoned together (we,—the Historian and the Professor) as we cast about for another knockabout journey.

Our "Club," so termed, had dwindled down to two, for various interests had separated us; but we found that there was more real work in this number than in any dozen chance would bring together.

When you come to think of it, is there any more real fun in a crowd than in a pair? And does n't it always happen that no matter how many start off together, they always separate into pairs?

Yes, "two is always company, three a crowd." With more than two, the company is always hauling different ways at once, and very little is accomplished, unless one wise head directs. In our case there were two heads, but we were united on one thing: we wanted to see all we could that was worth seeing. We wanted the best the world had to give in the way of wisdom and healthful pleasure. We had got tired of aimless wanderings, and had resolved that this journey should have a *motive behind it.* That motive was the study of history. Nothing so enriches the mind, broadens the man, and adorns the student, as the study of man's doings in the past. And to study the history of great events amid the scenes of their happening is the most fascinating of employments, and one that leaves the most lasting impressions.

We had resolved, then, to go to Spain *to study the history of America;* that is, to hunt out the homes of the early *conquistadores* (or conquerors), to examine the types of architecture we had seen reproduced in the West Indies, to visit Palos, whence Columbus sailed for America, Cadiz and Seville, the flourishing cities of that age, and the Alhambra, where the last of the Moors reared that palace so famous throughout the world.

Other objects we had also; but the central idea was *history*, and about this you will find grouped adventure and the incidents of travel.

In the first place, we 'd got to get there. We had thought it an easy matter to find a steamer going direct to Cadiz or Malaga; but when we came to scan the papers we found there was then no direct line at all, for the Italian government had engaged the steamers to carry troops into the Red Sea.

The next best thing was to go by the way of France or England. The best lines, we found, would carry us to Liverpool or London, whence we could purchase tickets to Paris, and thence to Spain. This we decided to do.

As we left America in March, before the usual tide of travel had set in, we had the best state-rooms on the steamer at our service, and at a lower rate than could have been secured later in the year.

Just where to begin, in a description of one's voyage and an

account of his experiences in a newly-visited country, is a difficult thing to determine. Were it an entirely new field, where no traveller had preceded, the task would seem comparatively easy; but in a country that has been visited by Americans time out of mind, what original thing can

EN ROUTE.

be said of it? And as to the voyage across the Atlantic, has it not been given a thousand times with details of wearisome fidelity, and the petty incidents of life aboard ship related *ad nauseam?* Verily, it is a troublesome task to write a fresh letter on an old subject. Let us state merely that the voyage across occupied nine days; that our ship, the good "City of Berlin," carried us safely. To be sure, the boat rolled about considerably, and disgusting old Neptune claimed and got his customary tribute. But, taken all together, it was a very satisfactory voyage, and we were not at all troubled to learn that the fast Cunarder, the "Umbria," had beaten us by nearly two days.

At Liverpool we passed happily through the hands of the custom officers and escaped without a feather ruffled. In truth, they troubled us far less than their cousins on this side of the water are wont, merely asking us to unlock our trunks, passing their hands over our goods in a perfunctory way, and bidding us go on. The only man who had his luggage at all overhauled was one Israel, a most suspicious-looking character, upon whom the officials pounced at once as a possible dynamiter, — the very man, in our opinion, the least likely to prove dangerous. We had heard so much about English extortion in the matter of fees from tourists and charges for cab-hire, etc., that we were prepared to undergo almost anything; and hence the reason, perhaps, that our experience, though short, was not so disagreeable as we had expected it to be. Thanks to an English friend, an acquaintance of the voyage, we made the trip to the station and thence to London at a minimum of bother and expense. Cabby, to be sure, asked a shilling more than his fare, but he did n't get it. Each one paid the porter sixpence at the station for trundling his trunks and valises off to the van, and we gave another hireling a few pence for thrusting some foot-warmers into our cars. On board ship of course we gave fees to the men who take care of the rooms and wait on the tables; and these fees are not obligatory, though customary.

We need not pause to reflect upon the railway system of old England, which is so excellent in its general features and so execrable in many appointments. To introduce a comparison between our cars and their obsolete carriages is like contrasting an ocean steamship with Noah's Ark. They were the usual old coops on wheels, into which we were shut with a bang at each principal station and left to endure the miseries of the journey to the next. The day was bitter cold, and with nothing but the iron foot-warmer to bestow heat, we were in an unenviable state by the time we reached London. In that city again the scene at Liverpool station was re-enacted, — a small fee to the porter, a sharp bargain with Jehu, and a ride through the crowded streets to Victoria station. As our train for Paris did not leave for several hours, my friend, though just home from a journey half around the world, proposed to take us about a bit; and after he had lunched with his family we returned for him and made a visit to the army-and-navy stores and other establishments, where, through his introduction, we had opportunity to purchase some needed articles at British prices.

It began to snow at dusk, and as it was not a good time, nor our desire great for sightseeing, we took the first train out for Dieppe. Of the routes to Paris, we had chosen that *via* Neuhaven and Dieppe for various reasons.

We were assigned seats in a compartment with six women, and then the door was locked, and those women began to chatter. The train was a slow one, and occupied three hours in getting to Neuhaven, but it arrived before those women had got done talking; and when they concluded the conversation we don't know, as we saw them no more. Through mist and falling rain we groped our way over a bridge across the railroad track to the boat, and dispersed ourselves according as we held first or second class tickets. Then it was ascertained that the boat would not leave till two o'clock in the morning. There were no berths to sleep in, but the first arrivals in the saloon (so called by courtesy) might possess themselves of a section of an upholstered bench, and stretch themselves out to sleep — if they could. The people on board seemed to take it for granted that we were all to be sick, but in this they were grievously disappointed. We crossed the famous and awful channel without being in the least distressed.

At Dieppe, where we arrived about nine o'clock in the morning, we found quite pleasant weather to welcome us, after the cold and snow of England; still, an overcoat was quite agreeable, and warm gloves were not unacceptable. There, also, for the second time, our luggage underwent the formal farce of an examination, — that is, we all marched up the street, carrying our hand-luggage, and had it "chalked" as fast as we could be pushed through a circuitous passageway at the custom-house. Then we marched back down the street in search of the cars and of breakfast. The former we found, and depositing the small articles in our seats, sallied out for something to eat. This excursion was tolerably successful, notwithstanding our limited stock of French words on hand, and the limited understanding of the waiters. While we were waiting for the train to start, a peasant girl came along with some apples to sell, — the smallest, most insignificant apples we had seen in a twelvemonth. But she assured us they were " ver grand appels," and though we would not buy, she insisted on giving us a bunch of flowers; which stratagem of course had the desired effect, and we purchased several of "ze grand appels," and had the pleasure of finding them as sour and worthless as they appeared.

On our way through England over the Northwestern Railway we were impressed with the thorough cultivation everywhere shown. Every rod of the surface seemed to have been ploughed, or harrowed, or grubbed with a hoe, or teased with a rake. But in France, on the route from Dieppe to Paris, every foot, every inch almost, seemed to have been thoroughly pulverized and planted. Thrift and contentment here dwelt side by side.

The ride to Paris was tolerably rapid, but four stops being made, — one of these at the celebrated Rouen, which has such a famous cathedral. It is not our purpose to give descriptions of French towns and cities, since all these can be found in the guide-books. When we once get off the beaten track, then we shall hope to present something of interest. We rolled into Paris through a drizzling rain, and escaped from the collectors of customs and *octroi* without any trouble whatever.   The customary question is, "Have you any spirits or cigars?" If you answer in the negative, and happen to have a fairly honest expression on at the moment, the chances are that your baggage will not be troubled.   As we had burdened ourselves with a trunk, owing to carrying numerous photographic plates and apparatus, we were compelled to pay well for the convenience.   In London they

made that trunk weigh one hundred and ten pounds, though we could have sworn it did not exceed eighty, and charged at the rate of five cents per pound for all in excess of sixty pounds. Thus we paid two dollars for alleged excess, and subsequently much more.

Well, we arrived at the Garé de Lazarus, in Paris, and took cab for our hotel.   Paris was gloomy, unattractive, cold and clammy, hence we did not linger long within its precincts.   In truth, we only went to Paris because we had to, in order to take rail for the country con-

A FRENCH BONNE.

tiguous to Spain.   We lingered there long enough to present a few letters of introduction, to find out that our friends domiciled there were as much disgusted with the city as we were, — on account of the weather, — then hastened away for the country more to the south.

We found out, however, that our French and the Parisian were not one and the same thing, that the people would persist in misunderstanding us, and that the best thing we could do was to run away and leave them to themselves. It is not necessary that one should speak French, however, to get about in Paris ; for in the centre of the capital there is a very numerous English population ; more or less a floating population, perhaps, but nevertheless always willing to lend a hand to a benighted foreigner unacquainted with the language. It may be that we were too sensitive, and because our own French rather grated on our ear, attributed to the Frenchman an aversion to hearing it spoken equal to our own. The Frenchman is very willing to overlook mistakes ; and many of the shopkeepers even will advance half-way to meet a foreigner, with a sort of provisional and extempore *volapuk* that would make one unhappy to meet with later on in his career. Some of the French terms are quite like our own, as for instance, " bifstek," which one might recognize on a bill-of-fare a rod away ; " rosbif " is another result of an attempt on John Crapeau's part to domicile some of our household words.

After all, Paris is n't such a bad place to stop in at the right season of the year. One can live there, also, as cheaply as in Boston or New York, if he so desires. Good rooms can be hired at very good hotels at from three francs up, and a meal can be got at almost any price. At " Duval's establishments " one can get a breakfast or dinner at anything above a franc. *Vin ordinaire* ten centimes a pint, beefsteak with potatoes fifteen cents. beefsteak with mushrooms one franc. Think of that! Twenty cents for a steak garnished with fresh and juicy mushrooms such as we of the United States seldom find.

There was a mild excitement in Paris when we were there over the advent of Boulanger, who quietly slipped into the city at daylight one morning, and took up his abode for a few days at the Hôtel de Louvre. As we were returning to our hotel one evening, we suddenly found ourselves in the centre of a noisy crowd, mostly of young men and boys, who were giving occasional shouts for Boulanger. All at once, from several side streets, bodies of gendarmes came charging upon the crowd, we were jostled from the sidewalk, and some of the boys were carried off to the "cooler." It was a rather feeble demonstration, but the only exciting thing we saw.

Having reached Paris, the next thing was to get from Paris to Spain. For a time we were in a quandary; but all at once it was settled for us in a twinkling. One day at the café we met a white-haired old gentleman, with a benevolent face and portly form, who introduced himself as an American long time domiciled in Paris, and perfectly acquainted with the language and customs of the people. This welcome acquaintance placed himself at our disposition, and gave us at once the very information we desired.

"It is just as easy," he said, "to go from Paris to Madrid, as from New York to Boston, after you are acquainted with the lines. The system of railways in Spain is French, for it was mainly French capital that built all the lines, especially those of the North and the international lines. These railroads cost immense sums, and their history is but that of roads the world over, — that which one company plants another gathers the fruit of. The northern lines especially are built through a mountainous country, necessitating numerous tunnels and bridges, and the road-beds throughout Spain are of a better grade than the average railroad throughout the United States. Instead of scattering a few cartloads of pebbles along a graded way and calling it a 'stone-ballasted' track, as is prevalent in America, these Spanish and French engineers build a good solid bed of rock and lay the rails upon a secure foundation. Not only have the French railroads penetrated into southern Spain, and even to its southern seaport, but they have leaped the Mediterranean and run down into Africa, even toward the great and dreary desert.

"The chief railway lines are the 'Ferro-carril del Norte' and the 'Ferro-carriles de Andalucia.' Two lines enter Spain from France:

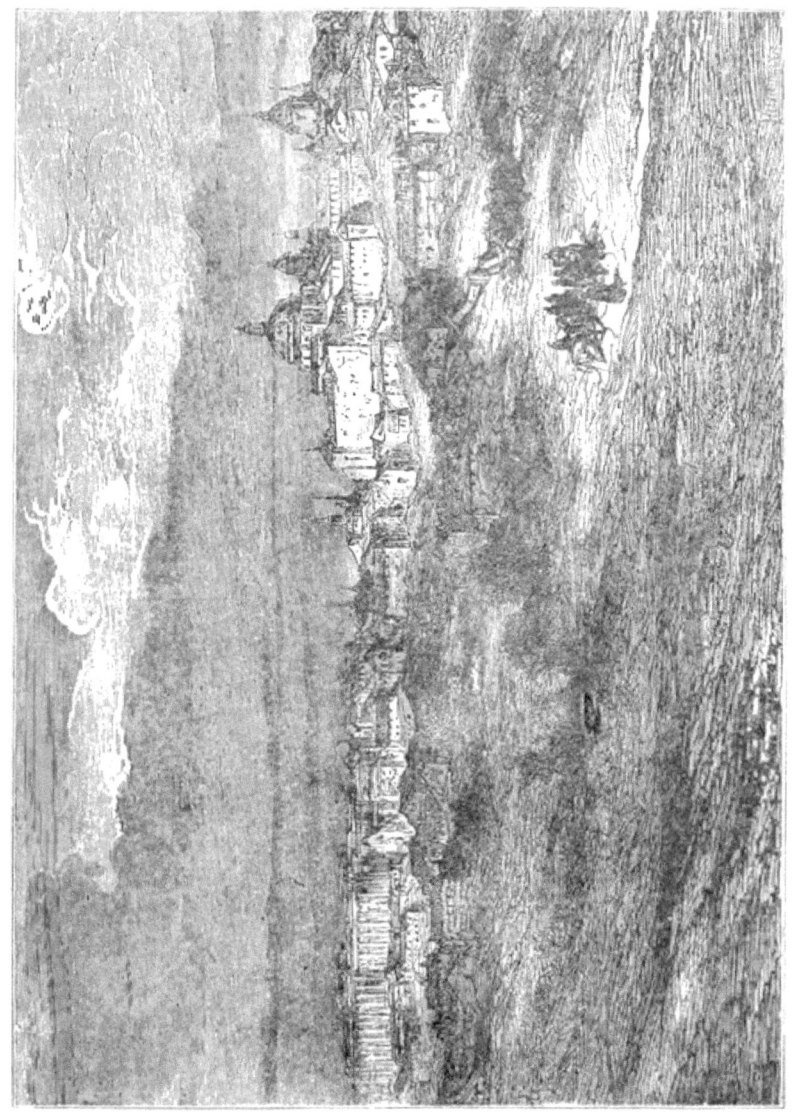

MADRID.

the most direct to Madrid being that *via* Biarritz, Irun, and Hendaye, and the other gathering together the various lines of southern and eastern France, and converging at Barcelona. Thence a line runs entirely to Tarragona, Valencia, and Murcia, connecting with cross-country lines for Madrid; a line from Barcelona to Madrid, — the direct coming down through San Sebastian, Burgos, and Valencia, for Madrid, other laterals branching off at Palencia for Oviedo and Corunna on the Bay of Biscay and the Portuguese system; an easterly line for Portugal, two southeasterly *via* Ciudad Real and Badajos. The Andalusian system runs southerly through Cordova and Seville to Cadiz, with branches right and left at Huelva, Granada, and Malaga. With railways constructed and projected, Spain is already well covered with a network, in connection with the Portuguese system, that enables one to reach nearly every desirable section of the land.

" Much riding may yet be done in diligences, if one likes that kind of travelling; but for my part, if any place can be reached by rail, I avoid the diligence. Some towns and cities can be reached only by diligence, such as Guadix, Baza, Alhama, and Ronda; but it is pleasanter to attempt them by horseback trips, or on donkey-back, than to take the discomfort of that conveyance. The average speed of the railway trains is about fifteen miles an hour; of the express trains nearly twice that. The diligence aims to cover some thirty to forty miles a day, the rate of speed being about a league an hour. Dear as is railway travelling in Spain, it is much dearer by diligence, much dirtier and dustier. Horseflesh — that is, the sort on hire in every town — is very cheap A horse for an all-day jaunt in Granada costs a dollar, or a dollar and a half, while a donkey would rent for about sixty cents. With a horse or donkey you will generally need a boy or man as guide and hostler, and his services cost about the same as those of the beast. Entertainment for man and beast in the towns and villages is quite cheap, both as to price and quality, the *mesones* (or hostelries) giving little attention to the stranger, and expecting scant remuneration."

We saw that our new friend the Judge was of that loquacious kind that likes to give you good measure for your money; but as he was giving us very valuable information, we let him run on. The Professor finally managed to squeeze in the important question : " How do we reach Spain from Paris ? "

"Oh," said the Judge, "as to reaching Spain; if there were a direct line from America to Cadiz, that would be the best winter route, or even if there were a respectable line to Bordeaux. The only steam lines to be depended upon are the English to Liverpool and other ports, and thence through France. The Inman line, with its new boats, now offers probably the best opportunities for crossing the ocean, and it is to be regretted that one equally good is not established between New York and the ports of southern Europe. The more southern the route, the shorter it is and the smoother the sea. I met in Algiers two gentlemen who had just

TALLY-HO.

made the voyage from Brazil to Spain *via* the Azores and Portugal, and who had smooth seas and summer airs (in March) the entire voyage. Taking Paris as an objective point, one may here find for sale a great variety of excursions, including Italy, Algiers, Spain, and Portugal, at prices varying from sixty dollars to three hundred. These tours are carefully arranged, offering a great number of combinations, and at prices about two thirds the regular rates. If you will come with me to Rue Scribe, I will introduce you to a ticket-seller who will give you any itinerary and route you wish, and you can leave to-morrow — or to-day, for that matter."

So with the Judge we went along, and in half an hour had selected our line of travel, bought our tickets, and were on our way back to the hotel to pack for Spain.

CHAPTER II.

N a Saturday evening, just as Paris was beginning to feel the tag-end of a rude blizzard that must have wandered across the Atlantic, we took a cab for the station and boarded the night-train for Bordeaux. As we went up to the window to have our tickets viséd, a silver-haired gentleman stepped in front of us and ordered a ticket for Madrid. Then he turned and confronted us with a cheery smile; for it was none other than our new and valued friend the Judge.

"Going to Madrid?" we both asked him at once.

"Yes; at all events, as far as San Sebastian."

"Then we can go together?"

"Of course. I'm going along to look after you, — that is, with your consent. Having been in Spain years ago, I think I can be of service to you."

We were overjoyed, and full half the terrors of the journey vanished at once before the cheery countenance of the Judge. Our luggage was duly registered, our numerous valises, "grips," etc., stowed away in the racks, and after the guard had closed the door we found we were locked in for the night; in fact, we were only let out at daylight next morning, when the train halted for a rest of less than five minutes.

The entrance into Spain *via* Bordeaux and Irun is more direct than *via* Barcelona, being a long night's run, say thirteen to fifteen

A SPANISH DILIGENCE.

hours, from Paris to the frontier. Just as the landscapes become most pleasing, as we reach the provinces south of Bordeaux, we are about preparing to leave La Belle France, and at Bayonne our Spanish journey looms ahead of us.

The grand watering-places of the trans-Pyrenean Spaniards is that delightful little Biarritz, with its three sandy beaches, its attractive scenery, and delicious climate. All the Madrileños who don't come up to San Sebastian for sea air, come to Biarritz. The last town on the French frontier is Hendaye, on the banks of the Bidassoa, where all passengers change cars, the French and Spanish railways being of different gauge. The Spaniards are not in such terror of invasion from France as the English; but they would not let the French engineers run an unbroken track from Paris to Madrid, so they astutely stipulated for a broader gauge than in France, and with this concession the Gauls built the road as they liked. In the river Bidassoa, which here separates France and Spain, is the Isle of Conference, where in 1660 Louis XIV. met Maria Theresa a few days before their marriage. Several other royal marriages were negotiated there, and in 1526 Francis I. of France was exchanged here for his two sons as hostages, by Charles V. of Spain.

The first town over the Spanish line is Irun (pronounced here *Ee-roon'*) where the Spanish customs officials make a pretence of "going through" your luggage. No passport is demanded, and the detention from the officials is slight. The scenery through this section is soft and pleasing, and especially so around Hendaye and Biarritz. The distance from Irun to Madrid is 397 miles, and the fare, first class, is 73 *pesetas;* second class, 55 *pesetas.*

The nearer we approached to Spain the more valuable appeared to us our new friend the Judge. In truth, he became all but indispensable. We were of course well provided with guide-books, phrase-books, and Spanish grammars; but the Judge was a veritable walking dictionary, and always had ready at hand just what we desired most to know. At this juncture his observations on the monetary system of Spain were most timely, as follow below.

"A person can do Spain," he said, " 'hook or crook,' in a few weeks.

AGUADORES

Indeed, I think a certain American lady wrote a book on 'Ten Days in Spain,' which contained, by the way, more information about the authoress than about Spain, — as was to be expected. The money you will be called upon to deliver will be Spanish silver; gold is seldom seen, though bank-notes are extensively circulated. To an American, the monetary system of Spain is simplicity itself, but to an Englishman it is troublesome. The *peseta*, a silver coin worth twenty cents, is the unit of value, and this contains four *reales*, or one hundred *centimos*. Five *pesetas*, or twenty *reales*, equal one *duro* or dollar; and these with the *escudo*, or half dollar, of ten *reales*, comprise the current silver coins. Many local terms remain to designate coins, especially the copper. A *cuarto* is about half a cent, two *cuartos* being equal to one cent or five *centimos*, while ten *centimos* are equal to an English penny. The people have their own peculiar terms; as, for instance, the double *cuarto* is sometimes called a *perro gordo*, or 'fat dog,' while the small *cuarto*, called also the *cuartilla*, is locally known as *perra gorda* (feminine 'fat dog'). Why these queer distinctions nobody knows. I remember how puzzled I was the first time I heard the *cuarto* called a *perra gorda.* It was one day in the elm-grove of the Alhambra: a gypsy girl passed me, and holding out a rose, said I could have it for a *perra gorda;* and I of course bothered over it a long time before I perceived her meaning."

In this connection, and for the guidance of all who may follow in our footsteps, we will add some useful hints regarding travel in this country so little known in America.

"As to the safety of the traveller in Spain," continued the Judge, "there is perhaps no other country where it is better assured. I was most agreeably disappointed in my first visit, having been told such stories regarding the brigands and bandits that it was with great reluctance I left behind me, at home, my old and well-tried revolver. It had been carried by me in Mexico, as also in the West Indies, and I was somewhat attached to it; so when told that fire-arms were the first things confiscated by the customs authorities when searching trunks, I decided to leave it at home. Many a time, in thinking the matter over, did I regret not having taken it, especially as the authorities never ransacked my trunk, and showed no disposition to confiscate. But, as it turned out, the revolver would have been a useless burden, and was better off in the States. Though I have been in many places that offered every opportunity for robber and cut-throat, I have always met with civility and a degree of hospitality.

"It is one thing to sit down calmly and speak of travel after you are nearly over with it, and another to write in the heat of the conflict with obtuse ticket-agents and obstinate porters. The general continental railway system of itself is sufficiently exasperating to an American, and it takes him some time to get adjusted. The obsolete coaches, the officious guards, the snail speed of the trains, and the indolent manner of doing business, — all these combine to make the whole thing appear ridiculous.

"To this day, the people of the continent stand in dread and awe of the railway system, and especially of the railway trains. They, one and all, view it as some great monster that has somehow got into the land, that is going up and down, taking them to different points at its own pleasure and on sufferance merely. What favors it grants them the poor public accept with gratitude and bow their heads, even hide their faces at its approach. Their anxiety to be on hand for the train at least an hour before its time of departure is something ludicrous to a stranger, — until he ceases to become a stranger and has dwelt on the continent a little while; then he too is pervaded with the same anxiety. After a while I found that I had become afflicted with the same disease; that if the train was to start at seven the next morning, I was quite restless all the night and must have my breakfast at five. If I could not get to the station at least half an hour before the train was due to leave, and have my luggage weighed and registered twenty minutes before the whistle sounded, I was in a state of feverish anxiety, only allayed when safe in my seat and the door of the compartment closed to all outsiders. Notwithstanding, however, the demonstrations of the excited travellers, the railway officials themselves never allow anything to accelerate their movements. The ticket-seller waits till the last moment before he throws up the window, and then he is not ready for business; he must first light a cigarette. When that is well alight, and after he has taken a puff or two, he turns languidly toward the window, draws in your money, looks it over, tweaks the bills or rings the silver on the ledge, then hunts around for the ticket you ask for, gives you your change, passes the compliments of the day with you, bows, waves his hand politely, and then turns to his cigarette, at which he puffs a little before serving the next in line. The Spaniards, I am bound to say, are very patient under this infliction, knowing that in the same position and under the same circumstances they would act in precisely the same way.

"With your ticket (*billete*) in your hand you hunt up your trunk (*baul*) or valise (*maleta*); and a porter, with his number in brass letters on his cap, generally stands ready to aid you. Give him your ticket and he will seek out the trunk, get another official to weigh it, and motion you to the little window of a little office, inside which sits the master of ceremonies, who takes the weight given him by the porter, enters it in a book, writes on a slip of paper the weight, charge, and number, and gives this to you along with your ticket, at a cost of a penny for registering, together with excess of luggage; this you pay, and then gather up your small things (unless in charge of a porter) and go into the waiting-room, — the *sala de descanso*. To check your baggage is *registrar* or *facturar*, which operation is complete when the 'dab' is on the trunk. It is then perfectly safe, and you can claim it at your destination whenever you like, a charge of not more than a penny a day being made for storage.

"This is a slow process, to be sure, but a long way in advance of the English, who don't give you any receipt at all, and slam your luggage around as though it never had an owner, and was part of the general wealth of the nation. Though the English are more liberal in the amount allowed than the French and Spanish (and especially the

Italians, who are not yet civilized enough to allow anything), yet they give you no security whatever for your 'boxes,' but are as ready to turn them over to any one else as to the lawful owner.

"Your ticket carries sixty pounds of luggage, first or second class, and all over that will cost you from *ten to twenty cents per pound*.   In my last journey from Madrid northward my luggage was found to exceed by a fraction less than two pounds, and the baggage-master kindly allowed me to open my trunk and pocket that excess while it was in the station.

"I do not recall any apparent attempt on the part of the officials to extort money from me by alleged overweight; but the rules they are

A FISH-BOY.

A TERRIBLE FALL.

obliged to observe seem to allow them no discrimination in the matter. In my case, it was only the weight of a Spanish dictionary that made the difference between the prescribed weight and excess. In America, of course, no question would have been raised over such a trifling difference ; but it is useless to attempt to ridicule these Spaniards out of their notions of duty ; an excess is an excess, and they calculate it to a fraction, according to the printed rules sent out for their guidance. You can take as much luggage into the car with you as you can carry in both hands, with a stout porter to assist you ; and the porter, though an official of the road, will calmly stow away for you in the racks and on the seats and under them, a hundred weight of baggage, without a murmur, provided you press his palm with a *real* as he leaves you. Custom, merely, guides these people ; and as it is the custom to charge excess on everything carried in the baggage and over sixty pounds in weight, so it is customary to admit twice that weight with passengers in the coach, provided it be not in the shape of a trunk.

" I will not deny that I have remonstrated with those hard-headed officials, and hurled at their heads some of the hardest words in this language, — for what is the good of a language if you can't fling it around occasionally ? — but I have long since seen the futility of it. So now I pack all my heavy articles in the valises and ' grips,' and let the porters do the hard talking. ' Ah, señor,' they would say to me, with a waggish tip of the head, ' *la maleta pesa mucho ; que pesa ! es oro o plata ?* ' — ' How much the gentleman's valise weighs ! is it filled with gold or silver ? ' "

As the reader may have already perceived, our equipage (pronounced *ay-kee-pah'-hay*) is likely to cause us much bother ; but, in view of the pleasure a well-stored trunk affords the " folks at home," when once it is landed and opened for their inspection, the little trouble by the way is as nothing.

" The mules and the diligence have for centuries been the great carriers of Spain, and a picturesque mode of travel it is, too. It is wonderful how the Spanish mules survive the blows with which they are overwhelmed. If they had only to bear the brunt of the *zagal's* blows, it would not matter; but the established usage of the country secures to them a large additional supply, and no one armed with a stick fails to contribute his share. The *zagal* wears a light and simple costume: a kerchief tied round the head, a colored shirt, cotton-velvet pants, a striped waistband, and sandals of spun flax. This functionary is always furnished with a supple stick, stuck in his waistband and carried behind his back, — like the wand of a harlequin, the badge of his profession.

" The *delantero* (or postilion) is thus named because he rides in front, on the leading near-side mule. He rejoices in the cognomen of 'the condemned,' as his toil is incessant. Formerly he spent forty-eight hours in the saddle, and at times more. He usually wears a cap of lambskin, which imparts a most savage expression to his bronzed face. The staff of attendants was formerly considered incomplete without the *escopeteros*, a name given to two gendarmes charged with the protection of the travellers in case of attack, and who, seated on the top of the coach, commanded the route.

" Throughout the entire journey the *mayoral* and *zagal* keep shouting to the mules, addressing them each by name, sometimes in friendly, sometimes in threatening tones, according to circumstances, in this style: 'Colonel, on arriving I will make me a cap of your skin.' Night does not stop the discordant sounds, and even when the *mayoral* had succumbed to sleep one heard him murmuring: 'Capitanaaa . . . comisariooo . . . raa . . . puliaaa . . . bandolero . . . arre carboneraaa,' etc., until he was quite overcome, when he was ably supported by the *zagal*.

" The diligence offers the most aristocratic mode of travelling, as it is only found on the king's highways. More correctly, its journeys have become extremely select, for since railways have furrowed Spain, this superannuated vehicle has almost entirely disappeared. Besides

A FAMILY PARTY.

the inconvenience we have pointed out, there is the constant danger of the coach upsetting; at such times the *mayoral* escapes by paying a fine of about sixty francs. Twice in our travels we were upset without suffering any serious inconvenience; but passengers are not always so fortunate. When travelling from Barcelona to Valencia we passed a frightful ravine, into which a diligence had been precipitated, carrying in its fall both travellers and horses.

"Having dropped some hints as to the mode of travel in Spain, it may be as well to mention the seasons in which it is best to travel. There is such diversity of surface and climate, that the visitor may suit himself as to either in whatever season he may arrive.

"As we generally seek a southern climate in order to get rid of the rigors of winter, this season is, all things considered, the best in which to visit the southern part of Spain. In autumn, the northern and western portions, working down toward Andalusia as winter comes on; for midwinter, Seville, Malaga, and the coast cities of the Mediterranean; but for possible rains, the early spring months for Granada and the hill towns of Andalusia. The months of April and May will be found well-nigh perfect in any part of Spain south of Toledo, with May and June for the more northern portions. The summer heat of Seville and such cities is intense, and no stranger should allow himself there at that time."

There! Now you have, thanks to the Judge, full directions for spending a summer in Spain. To return now to our journey. Our first halt was at San Sebastian. This is a beautiful little city of twenty thousand inhabitants, built on an isthmus at the foot of a high hill defended by a castle. It is the fashionable watering-place of Spain, bright, clean, airy, but wholly un-Spanish in appearance. The streets are broad, a tramline runs throughout the town, the hotels are excellent, and the people attractive. There is a good theatre here, a magnificent casino, and an apology for a bull-ring. In appearance the town is more French than Spanish, and even the language of the inhabitants does not readily suggest that noble tongue spoken a little way farther on; that is, among those you first meet at the station, such as the porters, hack and omnibus drivers, and hotel runners. For, though in Spain, we are in a portion of that country known as the Basque region, which contains the descendants of the oldest people of Hispania.

If we may believe the Basques themselves, they claim direct descent from Noah and Tubal, and have lived here, they and their ancestors, since the epoch of the great flood. It is conceded that the Basque is the primitive race of Spain, — an unconquered race. The Moorish invasion, somehow, and the Gothic, passed by them, and left them here with the customs, traditions, and language of earliest times. They are fine people physically, honest, hospitable (it is said), and truthful. Their customs and costumes are quaint, and proclaim their long adherence to a fixed place of residence. They are proud of their ancestry, many claiming a descent from noble houses, and great sticklers on ceremony. In the midst of the fashion and gayety of the visitors from France and Madrid these people preserve their simple ways, their ancient usages and games. The great game here, that is with them a passion, is that called *juego de pelota*, a kind of five-court, for the playing of which they have a fine ball-ground not far from the centre of the town.

Philologists affirm that the Basque language was once the universal idiom of all Spain, that there are at least two thousand Spanish words derived from Basque, and the Basques themselves are the remnant of its primitive people. It is said to be very difficult to acquire, and we are told that his satanic majesty himself spent several years in a fruitless effort to gain a knowledge of it. One writer says that the Basques seem to understand each other's speech, but that he does n't believe they do. For instance, "they will write Solomon and pronounce it Nebuchadnezzar." The Basques declare that theirs was the language of Adam in Paradise, and brought to Spain by Tubal. Humboldt,

who studied the Basque, believed it to be the ancient language of
Iberia (old Spain), and there are some who think it related to the Celtic.
Another, a French writer, affirms his belief that it is identical with, or
similar to, the speech of one of the Berber tribes of North Africa. At
all events, it is interesting, and is the one tongue or idiom that has
held its own in the various mutations of Spain. With the Bay of
Biscay at their back and the Pyrenees on their flank, the Basques
combine the characteristics of the hardy followers of the sea and the
sturdy mountaineers.

Quite unexpectedly we met with friends in the first Spanish town
we visited. Happening to bethink ourselves that there was an American missionary station in San Sebastian, we called to pay our respects
to the missionaries, and found that the Rev. W. H. Gulick and his
wife were from our own State, and that they knew many people with
whom we were acquainted. Without knowing whether we were
Catholic or Protestant, or indeed whether we had any religion at all,
they invited us to tarry with them awhile and take a look at the
Basque country. Needless to add that we accepted an invitation like
this, and that we thoroughly enjoyed every hour of our stay.

San Sebastian is a bright and attractive town, and advantageously
situated for an educational work like that in which Mr. and Mrs. Gulick
are engaged. For missionary work is educational, let it be called
what it may. In its very essence it is helpful, whether it proceed
along denominational lines or not. The work here undertaken is
educational in its best and highest sense, inasmuch as it operates
mainly among the poor and neglected. We wish our readers could
have looked in at the party gathered within the walls of the school on
the evening of our arrival. They would have seen such a gathering of
beautiful, bright-eyed children as would have warmed a heart of sole-
leather. We don't know how many, but a large roomful were assembled. The games they played, the poetry they recited, the songs they
sung, were all Spanish, but the music and mirth were in a language

universal, and alike infectious. A more delightful and thoroughly
heart-warming entertainment we never attended. The next day we
had opportunity to look in at the school in session, and were struck

NATIVES.

with admiration at the proficiency of the pupils, even in studies far
advanced. Some of the girls gave us a dialogue in English, and the
effect of this rough tongue of ours being caressed by lips accustomed
to the liquid and sonorous Spanish was most delicious. Their cal-

isthenic exercises were complicated (to an inexperienced eye) and perfect; limbs and bodies in harmony to music, and in rhythmic motion.

Sitting as spectators of these exercises, with those threescore happy children before us, the embodiment of health and happiness, with the intellectual sunlight dancing in their eyes, and the eagerness for knowledge manifested in their work, we allowed ourselves to speculate upon the possible future of Spain, with a thousand such influences as these working upon her masses. The people of Spain are a noble people: they have in them the material for great achievements; they are frank and sympathetic. They are not, like too many of our Northern races, sour and churlish; they are amenable to good influences.

There was one feature of the proposed work of this missionary station of which we may write with propriety, and that is, a projected summer school of languages and music. The situation of San Sebastian gives it a delightful summer climate, as well as winter, and a sojourn here between July and October would be in the height of the season. In order to raise a little money to assist needy Spanish students, Mr. and Mrs. Gulick propose having classes in Spanish, English, French, German, and Italian, and also in music. The terms, for board, lodging, and instruction, will be placed very low, much below the ordinary hotel rates, and thus a visitor may carry on special studies, while enjoying the delights of a Spanish seaside resort.

San Sebastian presents a good coigne of vantage for the stranger desiring to visit in Spain, as being so near the French frontier and yet with most picturesque and interesting country within easy reach. The finest natural feature here we have not mentioned, and that is the beautiful bay, called Concha (or Shell), circling round from the castle-crowned height above the town to another tower-topped hill just distant enough to give perfect background. The path up to the foot is one of the prettiest walks in the world, first through the old town along the hillside, then above the harbor-basin and through a forest of fine trees, at last out upon the breezy seaside slopes, with a view of the lovely bay beneath, and a glorious sweep of ocean beyond.

The seaside slope is thickly sown with graves, for here the French made their last stand against the English armies in 1813, before they were driven over the frontier by Wellington.

One of our excursions, through the kindness of our friends, and in their company, was to the little town of Pasage, from the land-locked harbor of which the great Lafayette sailed for America. The hills all about are beautifully green, dotted with white châlets, and the gardens are filled with the trees and flowers of a Southern clime.

The soft atmosphere of the South seems to bestow upon this region its delights, even though the rugged Pyrenees are not far away.

CHAPTER III.

NE might spend several weeks in San Sebastian, especially in the bathing season, and put his spare time into excursions into the country; for various diligence lines lead out, and the roads are fairly good. Pasage (pronounced *Pah-sah'-hay*) we have already mentioned, with its land-locked basin, surrounded by the quaintest of mediæval buildings, many of them belonging to the descendants of noble families, whose *escudos* (or coats-of-arms) are carved above the windows and doorways. The one street on each side the harbor is narrow and crooked. The people are primitive, almost archaic, in their customs and habits. We recall the old church, where we saw the floor covered with wax tapers in coils, each length of taper wound about a small tablet supported on short legs, and where the hundred tapers sticking up looked like the heads of so many coiled snakes. An old man was twisting cordage under the shadow of the church, and a group of washerwomen were having a lively time at a fountain in an angle of the road. We wandered through the cool streets, took photographs of the picturesque bits, and then retired to a café overlooking and overhanging the water, where we sat awhile and took in the beauty of the sunset-lighted bay. The place was famous for its chocolate and wafers; but we did not get any, because the girl delayed waiting upon us until our patience was exhausted and we left. Little scenes like this, simple, restful, full of happy incident, are part of our Spanish legacy. We love to dwell upon them, walk in imagination through the cool plazas, and converse again with the courteous, simple-minded people.

Striking southward from San Sebastian, let us gather up some

A FAMILY OF TRAVELLING MUSICIANS.

scattered links in the chain of cities leading to Madrid. At first, even for a whole day's journey by rail, the scenery is suggestive of Swiss and Alpine regions; the road leads through numerous tunnels, winds over hills and through valleys ; hills and valleys green and fruitful, the white houses of the farmers and the husbandmen gleaming on the hillsides. Not many cities, but forests of oak and chestnut, and broad fields of grain, with here and there a mountain overlooking, — such is the character of the central of the border provinces of Spain ; in the east they are more arid, and in the west more rugged.

Three hundred miles from Madrid we find Vitoria, celebrated in modern history as the scene of Wellington's great victory over the French in 1813, when he drove Joseph Bonaparte, nicknamed *Papa Bote* (or Father Bottle), flying toward the border, and recaptured immense plunder which the miserable French had taken from convents and churches. At San Sebastian Wellington put the finishing touches to his long campaign in Spain, and after great slaughter sent the Gauls back to France, never to return in the character of invaders again. Below the citadel of San Sebastian, on the hillside facing the sea, are the graves and tombs of the English soldiers who perished in that great struggle. It was a glorious victory for Wellington, but had an inglorious sequence, as the brutal English soldiery broke loose from all restraint, and revelled in lust and carnage, setting the city on fire, and outraging the defenceless inhabitants.

Above the town of Miranda, where there is a fine station building, are the ruins of a castle to which, tradition relates, the ill-fated Don Roderick, last of the Goths, brought the beautiful Florinda; but why he brought her here, or when, history does not inform us. The truth is, he did n't come here at all. The scenery grows wilder and more suggestive of stern Castilian character beyond Miranda, and in the gorge of Pancorbo we have that Cimmerian gloom that Doré delighted to sketch, and which he depicted in his sketches of Spain.

Little by little the green woods and pastures lose their freshness, the trees dwindle away, the hills take on a hue of sadness, and at Burgos, at least, we have entered upon the wind-swept plains that extend, with variety only of rugged, serrated hills and shallow rivers, to

4

and beyond Madrid. A city we did net visit, nor had much inclination to, though the founding of it and its early years were fraught with historic incident, is Leon, lying away to the westward of the main line to the Spanish capital, two hundred and fifty miles from Madrid. It has one of the grandest cathedrals of the North, and was at one time the centre of Christian power, whence went out the armies that arrested, then turned, then shattered, the forces of Islam.

Another city, on the railroad line one hundred and fifty miles north of Madrid, we cannot pass by without mention. This is Valladolid, founded in the eleventh century, and once the Castilian capital, — at least, the royal residence, at times, of some of the kings of Spain. Its climate is rather milder than that of Burgos, and more salubrious than that of Madrid, but it has the dead-and-alive appearance of the former, and the latter has sapped its vitality forever. Valladolid has interesting churches, many most magnificent, besides a museum of sculpture and paintings; though the royal galleries of Madrid eclipse these latter, and they are rarely visited by tourists. Historically, Valladolid has a hold on the world on account of the great personages who have lived, labored, or died here. Ferdinand and Isabella were married here Oct. 18, 1469; Columbus died here May 20, 1506; Philip II. was born here May, 1527, and here presided over, thirty-two years later (May 21, 1559), the first of the *autos da fé*, in which numbers of hated Lutherans were burned at the stake. He burned his thousands, later on, before his accursed life came to an end; but it was in Valladolid, in the Plaza Mayor, that the flame was lighted which spread all over Spain, destroying the best of its population, scorching its art and literature, lapping the life-blood of its citizens, and paralyzing its every industry. With one hand the great Philip builded, with the other he applied the torch, until we see the result to-day throughout Spain in the billions locked up in stone structure, useless convents and cathedrals, and in an impoverished population begging for bread in a land intended by God as the granary and vineyard of the world. From a wealthy city of one hundred thousand inhabitants in Philip's time, Valladolid has sunk to its present pitiable condition. Our interest in this place centred in the facts that Columbus died here and Cervantes at one time lived here. The house of Cervantes is said to be No. 11 in the Plazuela del Rastro, that where Columbus died, No. 2 Calle Ancha de Magdalena. It is a plain-sided structure, without a noteworthy feature, the most prominent thing upon it being the sign of a milk merchant over the doors: "*Leche de Burra y Vaca* [cows' and asses' milk] for sale here."

Six years the remains of the great admiral remained at Valladolid, in the convent of San Francisco, after which they were taken to Seville, thence to San Domingo, in 1536: and in 1795 were supposed to be transferred to Havana. The churches and convents of Valladolid are worthy of visit, also its library; but its chief interest lies in its mortuary memorials: in the death of martyrs to fanaticism, and in the death of Columbus, victim of a king's ingratitude. The gloom that surrounds it will never be raised, for it was so written by its founders and inhabitants.

Twenty-five miles farther south we reach Medina del Campo, the once famous City of the Plain, more celebrated now as the junction station of a railroad which will take us, going east, to the very ancient city of Segovia, and west, to the wonderful city of Salamanca. In the castle of La Mota, of Medina, Cæsar Borgia was confined two years, and Isabella the Catholic died there in 1504, says a reputable writer on Spain. It is related that when Charles V. passed through there on one of his journeys, a rich banker sought to do him honor by burning in the *braseros* (braziers) incense of cinnamon from Ceylon, then worth its weight in gold, instead of olive-nuts, which it was customary to use. The *brasero*, by the way, you will find in use everywhere in cool weather, generally placed beneath the table around which the company sits at meat or conversation, and sending forth charcoal fumes dense enough to asphyxiate a roomful of people.

While journeying on horseback to Salamanca our party fell in
with a mysterious-looking individual riding upon a splendid black
mare. As for himself, he was a powerfully-built, jolly fellow about
thirty years of age, wearing a costume not unlike that of an Andalusian
majo, while his *querida* was mounted behind him. It was not long
before we became friends with this bold trader, who when assured
that we were neither government servants nor *carabineros* (custom-
house officers), but simply *franchutes*, — such is the nickname given by
the peasantry to the French, — soon made us acquainted with some
of the mysteries of his daring craft. The first operation of the *contrabandista* consists in his proceeding to Gibraltar to lay in his stock
of wares. It is generally the Jews who supply him with the articles
in demand, — muslin, silk handkerchiefs, cigars, tobacco, etc. So far,
nothing is safer or simpler in trade, but the difficulty is how to introduce them into Spanish territory; but there is the *corredor*, who is
able to solve the problem. This agent is a person who has found
it necessary, on account of his peculiar peccadilloes, to take up his
abode in Gibraltar. The industry of this middle-man consists in
removing the obstacles which conscientiously-disposed customs officers might set up. A few *pesetas* here, and a few *pesetas* there,
silently dropped into the hands of certain ornaments of justice and
guardians of revenue, renders them unable to discover the contents
of the *alforjas*, or the nature of the articles concealed beneath the
aparejo of the mules. It sometimes happens that the *corredor* under-
takes operations on a much larger scale, on account of important
mercantile firms.

Our more modest *contrabandista* contents himself by taking a few
loads of silk handkerchiefs or tobacco, and as soon as he has crossed
the frontier he joins his comrades, and the caravan sets off on the
march, taking care to travel only at night, halting during daylight in
the *cortijadas* (or isolated farms), or in villages where they have trusty
friends. These hardy smugglers know all the most difficult passes

SMUGGLERS.

of the sierras, which they some of them cross with burdens on their backs and carbines slung over their shoulders, clinging with their hands to the projecting ledges on the perpendicular rocks. Strange to relate, these traders are often on the best of terms with the authorities of the villages through which they pass, never neglecting to offer a packet of fragrant cigars to the *alcalde*, tobacco to his scribe, and an attractive silk handkerchief to *la señora alcaldesa*. They almost always reach their destination without let or hindrance. Nevertheless, they are at times surprised by a band of *carabineros*, when they wake the echoes of the sierras with the reports of their *retacos*. This, however, is a very rare occurrence, as it pays better to settle amicably with their easily-pacified foes, who are always open to the magic influence of a few *duros*. Arrived at the termination of his journey, the trader delivers up his wares to his constituents, who sell them on joint account; but it sometimes happens that the tobacco and cigars are sold for the trader's sole benefit.

This daring adventurer, when not engaged in commerce, devotes his hours of leisure to spending with reckless prodigality the money he has gained at the peril of his life. He passes his time at the *taberna*, either playing at *monte* (a game at cards of which he is passionately fond), or in relating his adventures, taking care to moisten his narrative with frequent bumpers of sherry, *remojar la palabra* (to soften his words), according to the common Andalusian phrase. As might naturally be expected, and notwithstanding his brilliant opportunities, the contrabandist who does the work rarely accumulates a fortune, while wealth and honor seem to wait upon the *hacienta* with whom he shares his gains. He frequently ends his days either in prison or in the *presidio*.

We were assured that many of the smugglers, when trade was languid, took to the road and to lightening travellers of their baggage and money, — an operation always conducted with the utmost courtesy. It is just possible that this report only does them simple justice, as the profession of smuggler is a sort of apprenticeship to that of highway robber.

It is about forty miles to Salamanca, a journey that in days past necessitated much jolting in a diligence, but now performed in three hours. A dull and dreary college town is Salamanca, with only its prestige of greatness and the shells of its once famous university. But there is enough of interest here crowded within its confines to occupy one as long as he likes. As the world knows, the most brilliant epoch of Salamanca was the sixteenth century; for its university, one of the first in Europe, both in importance and in its foundation, dates from the fourteenth century. It was founded by Alphonso, ninth king of Leon, and was second only to that of Paris, ranking with Oxford and Bologna. A portion of its cathedral dates from the twelfth century, and there are several convents and colleges of the next and the fourteenth centuries. In the cathedral are valuable carvings, and among other relics, the veritable crucifix carried by the Cid Campeador at his saddle-bow in his battles. Of the several convents, all worthy of attention, perhaps that of San Estevan, or San Domingo, will attract the American visitor, since it was here that Columbus resided two years, from 1484 to 1486, when he was pleading for authority from the *catedraticos* for the promulgation of his views respecting the shape of the earth. He did not gain it, as the New World knows, and it was six years later that he did demonstrate the correctness of his theories by the discovery that brought consternation to the ecclesiastics.

Salamanca abounds not only in numerous buildings of a public character, but in private houses of ostentatious and beautiful architecture. Perhaps that known as the *Casa de las Conchas* (or house of the shells) is the most curious, covered as its façade is with imitations of shells. The river upon which the city is situated is crossed by a noble bridge of Roman foundation, of the time of Trajan, and carries us back to the ancient Salamantica of the Romans, and to the pre-Gothic period.

SEGOVIA ALCAZAR AND CATHEDRAL.

East from Medina del Campo about sixty miles is Segovia, anciently a Roman city, a fortified place, and with an aqueduct (likewise ascribed to the times of Trajan) as its noblest structure. It brings water from a point nine miles away, and has arches one hundred feet in height.

SALAMANCA.

The grand monuments of Segovia are three in number : the aqueduct the alcazar, or Moorish citadel, and its cathedral. The aqueduct is eighteen centuries old, the alcazar nine centuries, and the cathedral (built 1525) occupies the site of another dating its construction from the eleventh. Truly Segovia, with its fine old Gothic residences, its grand structures, and its commanding position upon a fortified hill above a' river, should not be passed by any more than Salamanca. Readers of "Gil Blas" must note that he was immured in a dungeon of the alcazar of Segovia; and lovers of the picturesque will need no other incentive to cause them to visit here.

Of grand cathedrals, the city of Palencia, on the road from Santander to Medina, possesses one of the grandest in Spain; and in speaking of seats of learning we should not forget that here was founded, it is said, the oldest university in Spain, one older than Salamanca's: and again, in Palencia (according to the romance) the great and only Cid was married to Ximena. The Cid — as we have seen — has been apportioned out pretty well; Burgos claims the honor of his birthplace, Salamanca has his battle-crucifix, Valencia plumes itself as the place in which he died; hence, like Burgos, it is also *la ciudad del Cid Campeador*. And yet, the Cid was not one who went about mindful of the proverb: *Miel en boca, y guarda la bolsa,* — "honey in the mouth, and a guard on the purse;" but was a swaggering, swash-buckler sort of a fellow, free with his money and free with his blows.

Of university towns, second to Salamanca only, — surpassing it in certain unique features, — is Alcalá, situated some twenty miles from Madrid, on the road to Zaragossa. A city of Roman foundation, it was not given a world-wide reputation until the great Cardinal Ximenes established here his university in 1510, which sprang into being almost perfectly equipped for its work, through the genius of its founder. The name Alcalá is derived from the Arabic *Al-Kalat* (the castle), hence is borne by several other towns once in the possession of the Moors, and to distinguish it this one is called Alcalá de Henares, from the river flowing by it. This ancient rival of Salamanca is now quite as defunct as that city, and less known to-day. Yet here was one of the most famous universities of its day (which existed until fifty years ago, when removed to Madrid), and here was undertaken and carried out the most stupendous literary enterprise of the age.

We refer to the celebrated polyglot Bible, the great Complutensian (so called from Complutum, the Roman name of the town), which was printed here in 1517. A copy is in the Biblioteca at Madrid. It is printed in the Hebrew, Latin, Chaldee, Septuagint, Greek, and the Vulgate, and the then known world was searched for the ablest scholars of the age, who were brought to Alcalá and labored here for years. This work alone would render Alcalá ever memorable; but it has another claim upon the world's attention as the birthplace of Cervantes, who first saw the light here in 1547, as attested to by the registry of births, still to be seen in the church of Santa Maria. Miguel Cervantes himself, probably one of the festive *estudiantes* of his day, wrote lovingly of Alcalá and student-life there.

We don't find them numerous now in Spain, those *estudiantes* who make the student-life a profession, and starve themselves into scarecrows, prowling about the country in jolly bands, each one draped in rusty cloak and carrying a *pandero* (or musical instrument). If they were not now so scarce, the public would not have such liking for the *estudiantes* who make a living by music at *fiestas* and fairs. The student of olden days is kept in mind by the songs he sung and the pranks he played as he serenaded the *señoritas* and raided the market-places. Here is something that epitomizes the student-life of Alcalá and Salamanca, which we will translate as well as we can:

> " Cuando un estudiante sale
> Al mercado, dia cubierto.
> Los jamones y los embuchados
> Se ponen en movimiento."

The following is a very free translation : —

> " When a student to the market sallies,
> On a day that 's overcast or stormy,
> All the noble hams and toothsome sausage
> Scramble for a place beyond his clutches."

From some needy student, we doubt not, came the following

lines, which breathe a philosophy none but a Spanish beggar could express : —

> " Los pobres mas hambrientos
> Son los mas ricos
> Porque todo lo comen,
> Con apetito ;
> No así los grandes.
> Que aunque todo les sobra,
> Les falta el hambre.

> " Those who are hungriest,
> Those are the richest,
> Because all they eat
> Is with appetite :
> Not so the great ones, —
> Though they have overplus,
> Always lack hunger."

The Judge and the Professor are responsible for this interlarding of Spanish proverbs and poetry, for they take delight in the odd and the curious. From old books and old people they collected these and the following, and now spread them forth for the delectation of their friends of the Knockabout family. Here is something about the Aragonese, who inhabit the province of Aragon.

"When an Aragonese is born, his mother knocks him on the head with a platter. Should the plate break, he is a choice, hard-headed child; but if not he is looked upon as a *soft-head*, and a probable cause of sorrow."

Like the Basque province, the Asturias was never subjugated by the Moslems.

We were annoyed greatly, in travelling from one city to another, by the frequency of the saints' days in the calendar, because our guides and porters insisted upon making them holidays, spending them in idleness. Not only the men and women, boys and girls, have their favorite saints, but all the lower animals, even the *burros* (or donkeys). Saint Anthony is the donkeys' saint : and on his day horses and donkeys are brought before a certain church and blessed, and small loaves of barley bread given them by the priest. Saint Anthony is also the patron of spinsters, for whom he kindly procures hus-bands when they desire them.

When a woman wishes his aid, she throws an image of the saint to the bottom of a well, and tells him to stay there till he has got her a husband. Many of the people have great faith in the stories of the saints, and in their ability to help them. Many, again, live in poverty to pur-chase masses for their souls in purgatory. Philip IV. ordered that one hundred thousand masses should be offered for him after death, to take him through purgatory; if he ceased to require them, then for his parents, and after they had ascended into heaven, for those who had been slain in the wars of Spain.

It is related that the Count de Villa Medina once gave a piece of gold valued at four dollars to a monk who, when he received it, exclaimed, " Ah! that releases a soul from purgatory." He gave him another piece of gold, and another, and another, every one of which, the monk declared, re-leased a soul from purgatory.

"Where are they now?" said the count.

" Safe in heaven, every one."

" Are you sure? "

" Yes; quite sure."

" Then," said the count, "give me back my money, for once safe in heaven they can never return."

But the monk kept the money.

Next to the priest, the *escribano* (or public letter-writer) is held in high estimation by many of the ignorant. This man can sometimes be seen on the corners of the streets or beneath a corridor with a table and inkhorn, ready to write letters for any one needing his services. It is said that his chief employment is in writing love-letters for *señoritas* as well as men; and about him the following lines are written, referring especially to his goose-quill pen : —

> " Pajaros con muchas plumas,
> No se pueden mantener ;
> Los escribanos con una
> Mantienen mozo y muger.

> " Birds with many feathers
> Hardly keep alive ;
> With *one plume* the writer
> Maintains cook and wife."

These specimens of Spanish doggerel are given in their own language, because they teach us so much of the habits of thought and the customs of the people. Let us now tarry awhile in a city where Spanish ballads had their birth.

BEGGARS.

CHAPTER IV.

AKING a long leap southward from the frontier, we enter Old Castile, and seek out the ancient city of Burgos, the birthplace of Gothic Spaniards, and the cradle of Spanish liberty. We took train at night, and then ensued the various incidents of a night by rail, — the broken naps, the confused awakenings, the hootings, tootings, cries, whistles at the stations; the intrusions of strange passengers who stumble over your legs, beg your pardon politely, but firmly possess themselves of the greater portion of the seat that you had fancied particularly belonged to you. So it was a very jumbled-up portion of a night that passed between the frontier and Burgos, and we were by no means sorry when the name of our destination was shouted out, even though it was five o'clock in the morning, and of a cold, blustering morning at that.

It was about a mile to the centre of the city, and to the hotel; a pleasant mile, we later found it, leading through long avenues of trees, along the banks of the river flowing through the city. Even so early as five o'clock in the morning the river-banks were lined with washerwomen, hard at work, scrubbing for dear life. Each woman had a washing-board made long enough to receive her knees and skirts, and over this she leaned, sousing the clothes in the water of the swift-flowing stream. We made a very good photograph of one of these groups, later in the day, with an old convent as the

background and the foaming water in the fore. A strapping maid
led us to our rooms, ordered coffee, and then left us to a nap of several
hours, after which we went forth into the city, which was then hum-
ming with active life.

We had prepared ourselves to see much in Burgos in the way
of fine architecture and historical monuments; nor were we at all
disappointed. It came fully up to our expectations, though of course
not exactly the city we had built from readings of history and travel.
Although the climate is not delightful, especially to one fresh from
the perfect airs of Andalusia, still the scenes about are not uninter-
esting. The usual prospect of north-central Spain, of broad plains
and rounded hills, rewards him who climbs to the castle, the cathedral
towers, or some other point of observation.

We fancy the Spaniards would be unable to give a reason for the
location of many of their cities, especially in the north, where they
seem to have grown from earliest times without any fitness of scene
or surroundings. The coast cities have a reason for their situation,
such as advantages of harbor or point-of-call for merchant vessels;
so too have many of the cities on rivers, such as Cordova and Seville.
But here the river is too small for navigation, nor is there any place
accessible which might be of importance to this by its contiguity.
We suppose that it presented some features for fortification or defence
in those early days when it was pitched upon for a settlement.

And what were those times, and wherefore was Burgos called into
being? "At the time of the general wreck of Spain, by the sudden
tempest of Arab invasion," says Irving, in his beautiful Introduction
to the "Moorish Chronicles," "many of the inhabitants took refuge
in the mountains of the Asturias, burying themselves in narrow valleys
difficult of access, wherever a constant stream of water afforded a
green bosom of pasture land and scanty fields for cultivation. For
mutual protection they gathered together in small villages, called
castros, or *castrellos*, with watch-towers and fortresses on impending

MONASTERY OF LAS HUELGAS, BURGOS.

cliffs, in which they might shelter and defend themselves in case of sudden inroad. Thus arose the kingdom of the Asturias, of Pelayo and the king's successors, who gradually extended their dominion, built towns and cities, and after a time fixed their seat of government at the city of Leon. An important part of the region over which they bore sway was ancient Cantabria, extending from the Bay of Biscay to the Duero, and called Castile from the number of castles with which it was studded."

After a time the Castilians " threw off their allegiance to the kingdom of Leon and elected the judges to rule over them, — one in a civil and the other in a military capacity. The first who filled the stations were Nuno Rasuro and Lain Calvo, two powerful nobles : the former descended from Diego Porcallo, a count of Lara ; the latter, ancestor of the renowned Cid Campeador." A grandson of Nuno Rasuro was Fernan Gonzalez, born about the year 887, whom Irving calls the " most complete hero of his time."

We are thus particular in introducing these heroes here, because their times were most critical in the history of Gothic Spain, and they took a leading part in stemming the tide of Moslem invasion. Here, in fact, the Gothic Spaniards made a stand not only for freedom, but for conquest, and with Fernan Gonzalez begins that long line of conquerors that extends in almost unbroken succession down to Ferdinand the Catholic and Isabella. For six hundred years they fought the Moslems, until the last descendant of the Arab invaders was driven over into Africa. And this movement for freedom began right here in Castile ; in this old city of Burgos lived the famous counts of Castile, who maintained perpetual warfare against the Moors. When Fernan Gonzalez was but seventeen years old he was elected to rule over his fellows, with the title of duke, or count, under the name of Alonzo the Great, King of Leon. " A Cortes, or assemblage of the nobility of Castile and of the mountains, met together at the recently built city of Burgos to do honor to his

installation. Scarce was the installation ended, and while Burgos
was yet abandoned to festivity, the young count, with the impatient
ardor of youth, caused the trumpets to sound through the streets
a call to arms. A captain of the Moorish King of Toledo was
ravaging the territory of Castile at the head of seven thousand troops,
and against him the youthful count determined to make his first
campaign."

He was victorious, killing the Moorish commander with his own
hand, and securing an immense booty, part of which was brought
back to Burgos, and part used in the endowment of a convent. Encouraged by the success of this engagement, Count Fernan kept his
soldiers and cavaliers almost continually in the field, extending his
conquests until a wide range of territory was wrested from the Moors.
He captured the fortresses of Lara, Mugnon, Salamanca, Carazo, and
the ford of Cascajares. His great successes brought upon him the
ill-will of the Christians, notably of Sancho, King of Navarre, with
whom he fought, and whom he killed in single combat. The son of
Sancho, Don Garcia, surnamed the Trembler, unable to cope with
Count Fernan in the open field, proposed an alliance with his family,
offering him the hand of his sister, the Princess Sancha; but when
the count went forth to claim her, attended by but a feeble guard, he
was captured by the wily Don Garcia, thrown into a dungeon, and
loaded with chains.

The Princess Sancha, learning that this noble cavalier was lan-
guishing in chains, and smitten with pity and remorse that one who
had come to claim her hand in honorable marriage should meet with
such reward, bribed the guards, appeared before the count, an angel
of light and beauty, and led him forth to liberty, after first securing
his oath that he would make her his wife as soon as they were safe
in Fernan's own domains.

So they went forth into the mountains, and after many perilous
scrapes and romantic passages arrived in safety at Burgos. " Vain

would be the attempt to describe the transports of the multitudes as Count Fernan Gonzalez entered his noble capital of Burgos. Princess Sancha also was hailed with blessings wherever she passed, as the deliverer of their lord and the saviour of Castile ; and shortly afterward her nuptials with the count were celebrated with feastings and rejoicings, and tilts and tournaments, which lasted many days."

King Garcia the Trembler came upon Castile with an army, but was defeated and taken prisoner, though subsequently sent home with honor at the intercession of his sister.

It was about the time of Count Fernan that the warring Spaniards first received material aid from the fighting apostle, Saint James. A great Moorish host came up from Cordova, so many in number that the plains were covered as with locusts. Count Fernan saw that the unaided arm of flesh would not avail against such overwhelming odds, and so retired to a hermitage on the mountain above the river Arlanza and prayed for help. In the battle that ensued, when it was tiding against the Christians, the glorious apostle, San Yago, appeared in the heavens with a great company of angels, and with a red cross on their banners. This was what the Spaniards wanted, and the Moors were dismayed at, for the latter retreated in confusion, and the former followed victoriously with slaughter.

If we may believe Spanish writers, the good Saint James has appeared several times at critical points in Spanish history and turned defeat into victory. At his appearance the soldiers gain courage and press forward with those inspiring war-cries : " Castile ! Castile ! San Yago and at them ! " Even in far-off America, centuries later, the soldiers of Cortez, of De Soto, of Balboa and Pizarro, were cheered by the historic war-cry of, " Castilla, Castilla and Santiago ! " Miracles were frequent in those days, it is said, but so invariably worked in favor of the Spaniard that our sympathies are enlisted in favor of the Moor, against whom they always operated disastrously, even though the Moslems fought stoutly, giving the Spaniards as good as they sent. For instance, behold what befell a devout Castilian, Pascual Vivas, who on the eve of a battle entered a chapel to pray. He continued so long at the mass that the battle went on without him, and he had the mortification of meeting his comrades returning victorious as he rode forth. Yet so pleased was the Virgin at his devoutness, that it was made to appear that he, Pascual Vivas, had been in the thick of the fight, his armor was indented, and his horse bore marks of the encounter, and his companions saluted him as the hero of the fight. It was explained that the effigy of Pascual had taken his place and enacted his part in the battle.

Well, the time came when the good Count Fernan approached his end, having lived a Christian life and having been always an implacable enemy of the Moors, from whom he had taken immense territories. They stood in such awe of him that his name was a terror, and the sight of the great silver cross, his standard, borne in the front of his legions, was always the presage of victory. This great cross, which is said to have been treasured up in the sacristy of the convent of San Pedro de Arlanzon, where Fernan caused his tomb to be reared, may have been taken by the pillaging French, as we did not learn of its present existence in Burgos, nor is it mentioned in the guide-books.

To-day we find memorials of Count Fernan throughout Burgos : a statue in the beautiful garden on the banks of the river Arlanzon, which divides the city, another in the great gate of the city, and an arch erected in his memory three hundred years ago.

The castle still stands, though in ruins only, in which Don Garcia was imprisoned in the year 958; where Alfonso VI., of Leon, was confined by the Cid; where King Ferdinand "the Saint" received the daughter of the Moorish king of Toledo, Saint Casilda, a convert to Christianity; and where Edward I. of England was married to Eleanor of Castile. This castle, the remains of which now crown the hill above the cathedral and dominate the city, was left in ruins

THE CID.

by the French, and is connected with the history of the invasion; but its main interest to the true historian is its connection with those times most ancient. True to their vandal sentiment, the French destroyed not only the castle, but by the explosion, all the beautiful stained glass of the cathedral, — an irreparable loss.

Two other structures bear in remembrance the early worthies of Burgos, and those are the Town Hall and the great city gate of Santa Maria. The Arco de Santa Maria is seen as you approach the city from the station at the end of a fine stone bridge. It seems a relic of the Middle Ages, with its flanking bastions of the ancient city walls, its turrets and battlements. The image of the Virgin stands over the great archway, and statues of Burgalese heroes; behind, a square away, but near enough to be quite effective, rise the high towers of the cathedral.

The Town Hall contains most ancient remains, and portraits of the founders of the city, and the earliest Counts of Castile. We were informed that the bones of the Cid were here preserved, and visited this place twice for permission to inspect these *huesos del Cid* and his beloved wife. A small party had collected by the time the custodian was ready to climb the stairs with us, and with true Spanish courtesy they pointed out the objects of greatest interest. There were excellent portraits of the Cid (conjectural of course), of Lain Calvo, and Nuno Rasuro, the old Roman chair (or Gothic) said to have been the seat of the judges a thousand years ago, and other relics. In a room specially prepared were the bones of the Cid, in a walnut casket, consisting of several long bones and broken ones. In a black glass bottle was all that remained of his wife, the faithful Ximena, she who was his support at home and the object of his affections.

Assuming these remains to be authentic, it seems a great shame that they should be thus exhibited. Any other bones would do as well, and any other handful of dust as vividly bring back to us the glorious presence of the renowned Cid Campeador. Better had they been left to moulder in the sculptured tomb in which it was the wish of the Cid that he and his beloved might rest forever. The empty tomb, to which the noble warrior was borne on his charger, and in which he and his wife rested for many years, may be seen to-day in the convent of San Pedro de Cardena, some miles distant

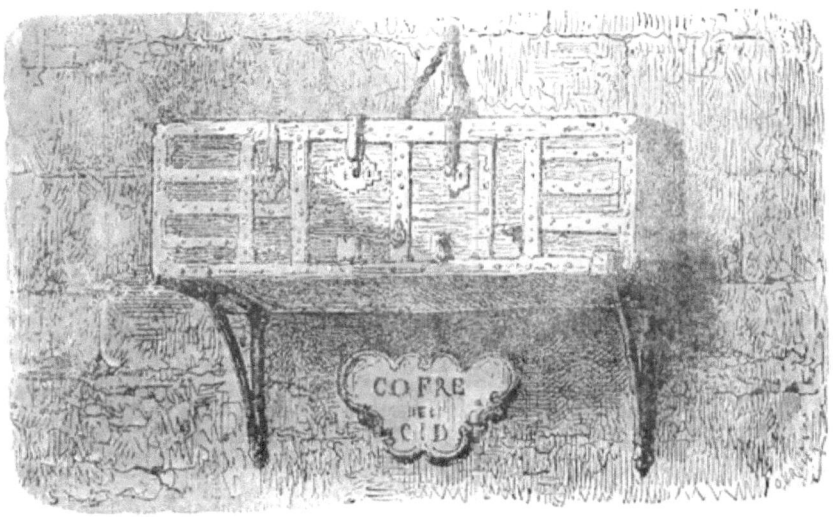

THE CID'S COFFER, BURGOS CATHEDRAL.

from the city. The sight of the *solar del Cid*, or his house, is indicated by three obelisks, which stand near the arch of Fernan Gonzalez. He was born here, it is affirmed, in 1026, and in this region many of his great exploits were performed. Some have affected to treat the Cid as a mythical character; but the Spaniards certainly do not, and it seems to us that the proofs are not lacking of his life and labors. He died in Valencia in 1099, whence his body was brought to the monastery of Cardenas.

In the numerous "Ballads of the Cid" the story of this hero's life is told; they are among the earliest of Spain. Here we learn of his first appearance as the avenger of his father, when he challenges to mortal combat and slays Count Lozeno. He afterward at the command of the king marries the count's daughter, Ximena, who has prayed her sovereign to be avenged, and who, strangely, consents to wed the slayer of her father. The king argued that "he whose hand had made her an orphan should of right be her protector; but how Ximena became reconciled we are unable to discover. That he was a model husband, the ballads inform us often, and we are told that he dearly loved his wife Ximena, his good sword Tizona, and his gallant steed Babieca.

He too, like Count Fernan Gonzalez, was a terror to the Moors. Knowing this, when he came to die, he commanded that (as a battle with the enemy was in prospect) his corpse should be set erect upon Babieca, his sword in his hand, and be led forth as he used to go in life, fighting for the glory of his country.

> " 'Bring in my Babieca,' — the Cid a dying lay, —
> ' That I may say farewell to him before I pass away.'
> The good horse, strong and gentle, full quiet did he keep,
> His large soft eyes dilating as though he fain would weep.
> ' I am going, dear companion, thy master rides no more,
> Thou well deservest high reward, I leave thee this in store —
> Thy master's deeds shall keep thy name until earth's latest day ; '
> And speaking not another word the good Cid passed away."

We may well believe that his friends complied with his request : —

> " ' On the death of Babieca, lay him deep within the ground,
> That never flesh of such rare worth by bird of prey be found.' "

Whether or not he performed all the valorous deeds attributed to his good sword, certain it is that Rodrigo de Bivar, the Cid Campeador, the hero of ballad and romance, was a personage any city might well be pardoned for claiming as its exclusive property.

In one of the cathedral cloisters you may see to-day an ancient iron-bound trunk which is said to have belonged to the Cid. Imagine it, a trunk over eight hundred years old! It is said to be the veritable trunk which he once filled with sand and pledged to some Jews as full of his jewels; but he redeemed his pledge, and paid his debts in full.

The general aspect of the city is ancient enough to warrant one in imagining its streets repeopled with cavaliers in mail and soldiers in armor. Some houses still stand of the fifteenth and sixteenth centuries, which are very quaint. The great Casa del Cordon, erected by one of the constables of Castile, is so called from the rope (or *cordon*) over the portal, which links together the *escudos* (or arms) of the houses of Figuera, Mendoza, and Velasco, with others of royalty. It occupies one side of a market square, and is conspicuous for its stone statues on the walls. The Casa Miranda is another, and the Casa del Conde, which bring back the gloomy Gothic of their times.

But the grandest building in Burgos is the great cathedral, begun six hundred and sixty years ago, and one of the first Gothic temples of the world. It is almost too grand to describe, with its noble towers three hundred feet in height, of beautiful openwork stone, its hundred statues, many tombs and chapels, paintings and tapestries. When we were there the cloisters were hung with most ancient tapestries of the fifteenth and sixteenth centuries, and there statues of Ferdinand and Beatrice looked out from their niches. Two miles from the city is a convent, built in 1493, where are beautiful alabaster tombs, and the high altar is gilded with some of the first gold brought from America by Columbus. Wherever we step we are reminded of things most ancient; and it is this flavor of antiquity that makes Spain interesting above all other countries.

THE INQUISITION, BARCELONA.

CHAPTER V.

E jogged along comfortably southward, thoroughly enjoying the scenery and the bits of Spanish life that we saw in the hotels and in the railroad cars. Whenever an especially dreary stretch of scenery appeared, or we suffered annoying detention, the Judge would draw upon his vast fund of Spanish tradition and reminiscences of former travels here. He delighted, like the rest of us, in the picturesque, not only of scenery, but of the every-day life. The beggars especially interested him; and many a story had he to relate about his encounters with them; for they cluster at every corner and squat by dozens in the porch of every church, dirty, deformed, persistent, and rascally. "Did you not notice," he said, "the curious helmet-like head-dress worn by many of the beggars of Burgos? Well, that is patterned after the helmets of the famous counts of Castile, the redoubtable knights who fought against the Moors for Spanish freedom. Yes, there is no doubt that many of those very beggars are descended from *caballeros* of high degree; and some of them possess, in their humble homes, *escudos* (or coats-of-arms) with quarterings that a prince might envy. Throughout Spain, indeed, helmet and armor of most ancient times are preserved to-day in the shapes of various Spanish costumes. There, for instance, are the *coletos* (doublets), the *abarcas* and *alpargatas* (or gaiters), and the *monteras* (or helmets). They are a curious people, these Spanish, a

strange mixture of goodness and cunning, of pride and gentleness. And the Spanish beggar is the most curious of all; moving in the very lowest stratum of society, yet always contented. The Spanish have a saying that with a crust of bread and a raw onion the beggar is perfectly satisfied : —

> 'Con pan y ajo crudo
> Se anda seguro.'

But ho! look out! There is the thing we have come so far to see; there is the Escorial, the Eighth Wonder of the World, — *la ochava maravilla del mundo*, the ambitious Spaniards call it."

We looked out the car-window eagerly, in the direction indicated by the Judge, and saw, rising from a hill, with a background of mountain behind it, the famous Escorial, with its gray walls and pointed towers. The Escorial is distant about thirty miles from Madrid, or a ride on the railroad of about an hour and a half. The guards shouted out the name of the station, and we all alighted and looked about us.

All the sight-seers had gone ahead of us in the omnibus, and the great courtyard of the convent was entirely deserted when we reached it, so that we were for a while at a loss where to go. Fortune always favors the dilatory, however; and so we fell in with a group of Barcelonians who were visiting Madrid and vicinity on a circular ticket, and who admitted us joyfully to their party. They were in charge of the official guide of the place, who was, or seemed to be, afflicted with some trouble of the brain, or total lack of sense, which made him an interesting though not an indispensable auxiliary.

Some of the guide-books will tell you that the Escorial was built in the shape of a gridiron; and the general plan of it does resemble one, with bars and handle, and towers sticking into the air for its feet. It took this shape, it is said, because of a vow of Philip II. to erect a monastery dedicated to Saint Lawrence, who was broiled on a

THE ESCORIAL.

gridiron, and would naturally be supposed to desire to commemorate this event. This Escorial is comprised of a monastery, a palace, a church, pantheon, library, and seminary. We enter first the great Court of the Kings (the *Patio de los Reyes*), two hundred and thirty feet long and one hundred and thirty-six wide, and see, at its farther end, six great statues of the kings of the house of David, the most noteworthy being that of Solomon.

Before entering the church let us try to grasp the magnitude of the entire structure known as the Escorial. It is a rectangular parallelogram seven hundred and forty-four Spanish feet long and five hundred and eighty wide, covering over five hundred thousand square feet. It is said to be the first great Græco-Roman edifice in Spain; and it were well had it been the last, for it is gloomier than a tomb, and severe to austerity, though grand and impressive as any artificial mountain of granite ever erected. Eight towers rise above the grand mass of granite to a height of two hundred feet, and the great cupola of the church towers above them all. There are sixteen courts (or *patios*), forty altars, twenty-six hundred windows, twelve hundred doors, eighty-six staircases, three thousand feet of fresco paintings, and eighty miles, it is said, of promenades, paths, walks, platforms, corridors. This vast work was begun in the year 1565, and was finished in 1584, having cost over three million dollars. One of the greatest wonders about it is, that he whose inception it was, King Philip II., should have lived to see it completed, and should have been able to finish and furnish it to the minutest detail, adorning it with the finest sculptures and the richest works of art. This was the fact that oppressed me, — that the mind of the gloomy king pervaded every part, and not a ray of sunlight or gleam of happiness that might be excluded did he allow within its walls.

The church itself, which is surrounded by the conventual structures, is three hundred and twenty feet long, two hundred and thirty wide, and with a height to the top of the cupola of three hundred and twenty feet. It is built in Doric simplicity, everywhere granite gloominess, heightened by its vastness. On three sides are chapels, including those of Saint John, Saint Michael, Saint Maurice, and the eleven thousand virgins. The organs are fine, but decaying; the frescos

"HARD LUCK."

are bold and beautiful. The pulpits of alabaster and gilt bronze are the only modern things here, and were the gift of Ferdinand VII. The high altar and oratorios are reached by a flight of blood-red steps, perhaps indications of the innumerable victims of its royal founder.

The high altar is directly over the pantheon, where lie the remains of Philip (all the Philips, in fact, except Philip V.), Charles V., and their families.

It was primarily as a royal mausoleum, in accordance with the wishes of Philip's father, and secondarily as a monastery, that this

ABDICATION OF CHARLES V.

costly pile was erected. The high altar is made of precious marbles and jaspers, inlaid, and the retable, or altar-screen, ninety-three feet high and ninety-four wide, is composed of red granite, gilt bronze, and jaspers, and cost over two hundred thousand dollars. It seems almost impertinent to speak of the cost of anything in connection with this grand edifice, as labor, money, treasure, art, even human lives, were lavishly offered upon its altars. The oratorios on either side the altar were for the use of the royal personages, and led to chambers behind and beyond. Above them are the celebrated effigies of the kings and the royal families, kneeling. These are of bronze; the groups on the right are Charles V., his wife, and female figures; on the left are Philip and his four wives, all portraits, it is said, and thus historically interesting. In the *relicario* (or reliquary) are said to be about seven thousand precious relics of saints, including a bar of the gridiron on which Saint Lawrence was broiled, and even a bone of this saint, with also one of his feet, a coal yet sticking between the toes. As Philip II. was the relicomaniac of the time in which he lived, and spared no money nor pains to secure the finest collection extant, he had probably the choicest assortment of holy mementos ever got together. These were all enshrined in gold and silver, with precious stones; but the French, eighty years ago, divested them of their valuable mountings, and left only the dry bones.

Although we had a guide who claimed to be the only and universal, yet we were obliged to leave him at every door and hire a special cicerone, either a monk or government official, to whom we were expected to pay a special fee. One of these led the way to the choir, with its carven stalls, its great lectern, or facistole, with the glorious choral books, over three hundred years old, each leaf made from a single calf-skin and beautifully illuminated. There seemed to be more than a hundred of these choral books, each one of enormous weight. We saw the stall in which Philip II. sat near his brother monks, where he is said to have received the tidings of the battle of Lepanto and the destruction of the Armada, — in both cases without change of countenance. In an anteroom is the famous and beautiful image of Our Lord Crucified, in Carrara marble, the work of Cellini, bearing the inscription : " Benvenutus Zelinus, Civis Florentinus facebat, 1562." It is a matter of tradition that this priceless crucifix, with its life-size Christ, was brought across Spain, from the coast to the Escorial, upon men's shoulders. Another ornament of the choir is a crystal chandelier, hanging near the facistole, which latter, though very ponderous, is turned by the slightest exertion of one's strength.

The one room of the buildings superior to all the rest, in the estimation of some of us, was the *sacristia*, one hundred and eight feet long and thirty-two feet wide, with fine frescos on its ceiling and celebrated

PHILIP II.

paintings on its walls. These paintings include Riberas, Zurbaráns, Guido Renis, Titians, Tintorettos. The largest, and in some respects the grandest, was a Last Supper by Tintoretto. A magnificent collection is this, even though presenting only the fragments of what it once was, the most valuable having been taken to Madrid.

It will be wearisome to describe all the treasures of this vast agglomeration of buildings. Let us merely mention the palace, with its suites of rooms hung with glorious tapestries, and with walls and floors inlaid with precious woods from America. Many of the tapestries were made at the royal factories of Madrid, after designs by the great Goya and others; but one hundred and sixty were from Flanders, fabricated after designs by Teniers. The rooms hung with these tapestries, which were mostly bright and cheering in tone and composition, were the bright spots in the gloomy pile; but these were of a later date than the time of Philip II., and principally brought here by the festive Charles. No one should fail to visit the Hall of Battles, painted over with wonderful battle-scenes between Moors and Spaniards, giving exact pictures of the arms and armor of that time, and consequently invaluable to the historical painter.

The heart of the edifice is a gloomy cell, where the master mind that had planned it went out from companionship with his filthy body on the 13th of September, 1598. The bare cell in which Philip II. expired opens out toward the high altar of the church, so that the monarch-monk was able to hear mass without leaving his bed. Here he died, holding the crucifix his father (whom he idolized, and whose commands he implicitly obeyed) had in his own fingers when soul and body parted company. His life here proved the sincerity of his declaration that he desired but a cell in the palace he had built to God. Builder of the Escorial, destroyer of the prosperity of Spain, slayer of heretics, who had lived to see the consummation of almost every gigantic scheme, he died as he had desired (but not in the manner he may have desired), in the building he had erected to cover the tombs of himself and his royal father. We saw a few relics of Philip in the shape of his stool, chair, and table, and the grooves worn in the stone floor by the moving of his bedstead.

There remain yet many things to see, but we shall only ask our readers to glance at the library. This also is of a grandeur commen-

INTERIOR OF THE LIBRARY OF THE ESCORIAL.

surate with the Escorial, the room being nearly two hundred feet long, broad and lofty in proportion. The cases are of choice woods, the books arranged with their edges toward the reader instead of their backs. The effect is strange, and of course unique. All are gilded, and have their titles inscribed on their edges. Many books, rich and rare, are buried here, including Spanish, Gothic, and Arabic manuscripts. Perhaps there are fifty thousand volumes remaining, after the spoliations of the thievish French.

We find here the "Codice Aureo," of the four gospels, in letters of gold, begun, it is said, under Conrad II., Emperor of the West, and finished about the middle of the eleventh century. Marble and jasper tables adorn the room, and a valuable old globe of the time of Philip II. We saw a MS. "Biblia" of the sixteenth century, and the "Codice de Oro," of date about 1050, the "Devocionario" of Isabella the Catholic and Carlos V., an "Apocalipsio de San Juan," Siglo XV., with pictures of gold and brilliant colors, on vellum. An illuminated Koran (Alcoran) is carefully preserved here and shown, and a curious "Vigila Mongi, o' Vigilanus," written in the year 976, illuminated on vellum at Toledo. There is also the "Tree of Love" (*El Arbol de Amor*), an illuminated vellum of *año* 1281. Another, Arabic, bore the inscription: "Muhammed Shams-el din Hapheth, Hegira 797 = 1400." Lastly, we found a book of Persian poems with illustrations in red and gold, that reminded us of pictures of the Forty Thieves, written by Ah Ben Muhammed, and a National History, in Arabic, bearing date, "Hegira 735 = 1358."

Well, the day came to an end. Our friends of the day strolled with us to visit the miniature palace called the Casita del Principe, with its pictures, gilding, ivory-work, and marquetry, and then they left us by the station, promising to meet us in Barcelona.

Our train did not leave till nine o'clock, and as the spell of the place was on us, we returned to ramble around the outside of the gloomy Escorial. We agreed with Amicis (an Italian author): " The Escorial is Philip II.; he is still there, alive and frightful, and with him the image of his terrible God. You remember all you have read of him, of his treasures, the Inquisition, and all becomes clear to the mind's eye. Then you would like to rebel, to raise your thoughts to the God of your heart and hopes, and to conquer the mysterious terror which the place inspires in you; but you cannot do this; the Escorial surrounds, holds, and overwhelms you; the cold of its stones penetrates to your marrow; the sadness of its sepulchral labyrinth invades your soul; if you are with a friend you say, ' Let us leave;' if you were with your love you would press her to your heart with a feeling of trepidation; if you were alone you would take flight. At last you mount a staircase, enter a room, go to the window, and salute with a burst of gratitude the mountains, sun, freedom, and the great beneficent God who loves and pardons."

We left our friends and took a path beneath the convent gardens, through a bit of wildwood and across a meadow to a point of rock which commanded the slope on which the Escorial was built, and the stern mountains beyond. This was the *silla del rey* (the seat of the king), where Philip came and sat at intervals to watch the progress of the great work. A little boy piloted us thither, and pointed out the hollowed seat in the granite and the groove beside it, in which the queen, Philip's wife, used to place her fan.

The sun went down as we sat there and gazed upon the great granite mass with its gloomy surroundings, and the shadows stretched across the valley before we descended. Calm and peace pervaded the scene as we walked across the meadows in the dark and silence, broken only by the tinkle of sheep-bells and cow-bells, and the song of a bird. Two white-robed girls were breaking down boughs of hawthorn as we crossed the meadow, and one of them looked up brightly as we passed; but she spoke not, and we kept our way on into the forest gloom, and thence past the gardens to the station.

THE ROYAL PALACE, MADRID.

CHAPTER VI.

SOME MIDSUMMER DAYS IN MADRID.

E were greatly disappointed in Madrid; but for this we were prepared by our readings, for hardly any one praises the city, and everybody has something to say against its situation. Witty and entertaining John Hay calls it a "capital with malice aforethought," inasmuch as it was deliberately founded here in the centre of barren and wind-swept plains, in obedience to the whim of a Spanish king. Except for the fact that it is near the geographical centre of Spain, there is no reason for it, as there are many older and finer cities better situated for the nation's capital. But here it is, and here it will remain, — a garish, uncomfortable, second-rate Paris, aping Parisian architecture in its buildings and Parisian fashions in its shops.

Much the city has, of course, that is attractive, and many things are here that no other city in the world possesses. Three centuries of time, the ambitions of various rulers, and the good sense of later legislators, have assembled here such treasures of art especially, that thousands flock here annually to inspect them. Take away from Madrid its museums, however, and little would be left.

Let us make a bare enumeration of the objects considered worthy of a visit, in this city of four hundred thousand inhabitants. First in interest, by all odds, is the Royal Museum, with its peerless collection of paintings; the Royal Palace, containing thirty large rooms on the lower floor, a grand hall of ambassadors, with velvet-draped and mirrored walls, and painted ceiling, with a gorgeous throne-room, the throne guarded by four gilded lions; a good library, theatre, chapel, and collection of ancient tapestries. The queen regent was living there, having just returned from Valencia and Barcelona, when we sought entrance; and as on occasions of the royal residence the palace is closed to strangers, we did not see the interior of the vast and gloomy pile. But we did see the guard-mounting, in the great court, and passed an hour quite pleasantly, inspecting the fine body of men appointed to guard the palace, the queen, and the heir apparent.

The present king of Spain, by the way, is a baby of four years, having been born after the death of his father, in 1885. Yet he is the recognized ruler over some twenty millions of people!

One of the buildings enclosing the palace quadrangle is more than locally celebrated as the royal armory, — the *armaria real.* Here we found more objects of interest than in all else of Madrid combined, excepting the Art Museum and the great Library. It is a complete exposition of arms and armor of every period of Spanish history, from the time of the Goths and Romans to the present day.

Entering the great room devoted to the armory, you look down a row of armored horsemen, with lance and helmet on, — a most impressive cavalcade in steel. They are of several different centuries, but principally of the sixteenth, when Charles V. and Philip II. were in their glory. Their royal officers in armor are here shown, mounted upon their war-horses; the famous Charles in that armor inlaid with gold in which he is depicted, in the Royal Gallery, upon canvas by the immortal Titian. It is stated in the guide-books that the armor of Columbus is preserved here, and that of Fernando Cortez.

In this connection we might mention that the armor of Boabdil, last king of the Moors, is in the possession of the Duke of Fernan Nunez, a descendant of his captor. This is probably the finest col-

lection of ancient armor and especially of that worn by historic
personages, in the world. We had seen that other great collection
in the Tower of London, and so had opportunity for comparison.
The two together give us a complete exposition of the weapons and

THE ROYAL ARMORY.

armor of ancient times ; that of Madrid being richer in artistic armor,
with chased and repoussé work on shields and helmets, and exquisitely-
inlaid designs in gold and silver ; and that of London in ponderous
flails and maces, cross-bows, cannon, and arquebuses. A visitor to
both armories will not fail to note how intimately connected were
the two countries, Spain and England, at certain periods of their
history. We were especially struck, in the Tower, by the appearance
of Queen Elizabeth, in her rich costume, mounted upon a horse,

and on her way to offer up thanksgiving for the destruction of the
Spanish Armada; and that was about three hundred years ago.

In Madrid is the armor, and also many portraits of that arch-enemy
of Protestantism, Philip II., once the husband of Bloody Mary,
whose portrait may be seen here. One end of the hall is covered with
trophies from the battle of Lepanto, where the last great Mohammedan invasion was checked, and Europe relieved of all apprehension of the hordes from the East. Banners and cimeters, great
shields studded with precious stones, and Oriental weapons of every
sort, are here displayed as memorials of that great and sanguinary
battle.

Although the armored knights on horseback are by far the most
attractive figures, bringing back to vision those heroes of Spain,
Gonzalvo de Cordova, the Cid Campeador, the Marquis of Cadiz,
Fernando the Catholic, Hernandez del Pulgar, Garcilaso de la Vega,
and a hundred other heroes of history and romance, not excluding
the great Quixote even, yet there are a thousand other features
worth observing. For instance, one may trace here the complete
development of the gun and musket, from the first rude matchlock
and arquebuse to the perfected rifle of the present day. We were
interested greatly in some richly-chased and gold-inlaid guns of two
centuries ago, with carved stocks of elegant shapes.

In the Naval Museum, contained in a separate building, is a
complementary collection of ancient and modern cannon, models of
the most famous ships and war vessels of time past and time present,
including those great galleons that voyaged to and fro between the
Orient and Mexico, Vera Cruz and San Domingo and Spain. The
great treasure-ships, once so eagerly sought, and sometimes captured, by Drake and Hawkins, and men-of-war that took part in the
conflicts of Trafalgar and St. Vincent, — these are all brought before us in the fine models in the Naval Museum. Going even farther
back than these galleons take us, into the history of Spain in the

THE FOUNTAIN OF THE CYBELE, MADRID.

New World, we may see in this museum paintings of the discovery of San Salvador by Columbus, and portraits of Colon, Cortez, De Soto, Balboa, and Pizarro.

A priceless memento of Columbus is preserved in an anteroom by itself, — no less than the great chart of his voyages, prepared by royal order, the earliest chart of the New World discoveries. The chart that Columbus himself drew, and took with him on his first voyage, is in the Columbina library at Seville, as well as his journal. We are reminded of Columbus in every part of Spain. In Seville is the slab that once covered his remains, and other memorials; in Santa Fé (Vega of the Granada) he last visited the queen before setting out upon his voyage; in the Alhambra he had an interview with his sovereigns, it is said; from Palos he took his departure, on his first voyage; at Cordova he passed years of waiting, while the conquest of Granada was going on. Madrid, at that time, was un-

known, but here, as the nation's capital, are preserved many memorials; at Salamanca he held that famous consultation with the learned doctors; at Burgos the high altar of the convent of Miraflores is decorated with some of the gold of his first voyage; at Barcelona, directly across the kingdom from the port at which he landed on his return, he was so proudly received by his sovereigns; at Valladolid to-day, we may see the house in which he died, and the convent in

which he for a time lay buried. The Spaniards, whatever may be
their faults, cannot with justice be accused of ignoring the claims
upon posterity of their departed great and worthy men.

We noticed, in this Naval Museum, a section of the tree of *noche
triste*, from Mexico; and this carried us back to that sad night when
the Spaniards were expelled from the city of Mexico with such terrible slaughter, and when Cortez himself fell down beneath this tree
of *noche triste* (the tree of the sorrowful night), and bewailed his
misfortunes.

> " In Tacuba, with Cortez, was many a gallant chief;
> He thought upon his losses, and bowed his head in grief."

The immense two-handed sword once belonging to Don Juan
of Austria is shown in the Columbus room, and many paintings of
ancient vessels. Very ancient and curious cannon are also here.
which take us, in imagination, back to their first use in Spain, and
hence in Europe. We read that gunpowder was first employed at
the siege of Baza, by a Moorish king, in 1312 and 1325. "More than
twenty pieces of artillery used at the siege of Baza," says Prescott,
in "Ferdinand and Isabella," "are still to be seen in that city, where
they long served as columns in the market-place;" and we were
told in Granada that some of them are there still. More artillery of
ancient date can be found in Spain, perhaps, than in any other
country of Europe, owing to the demand for it immediately upon
its invention, by the Spanish sovereigns, to use in their wars against
the Moors. But it has to a great extent been destroyed and recast;
and the French are responsible for the disappearance of a vast
quantity. For the French had respect neither for antiquity nor
historic association, in their invasion of Spain of eighty years ago,
and razed to the ground many of Spain's monuments, as well as
plundered her of richest treasures. Another museum, but of minor
interest, is the *Museo Arqueologico* (or archæological). There are

CARDINAL XIMENES.

several libraries, including that of the Duke of Veragua, a descendant of Columbus, the Palace library, and the National.

The *Biblioteca Nacional* (or National Library) has many famous books, including the earliest publications of the world. There we find the Forum Judicorum, the earliest code of Spanish laws, and illuminated manuscript of the eleventh century (1095), a Gothic ritual of the thirteenth century, in primitive Spanish, and a copy of the first book ever printed in Spain, or at least of the second. The first press (according to Prescott) appears to have been erected at Valencia, in 1474, and the first book printed in Spain a collection of songs in honor of the Virgin. The first classic was of the works of Sallust, in 1475. The book shown us in the Madrid library as the first print of the press was printed in Valencia, 1475.

"The claim of Valencia to the first printing-press is disputed by Barcelona, but to Valencia doubtless belongs the honor." Barcelona claims also, and it is thought with justice, to have been the first city in Europe to establish a bank of deposit, which it did in 1401. It was, we know, one of the most ancient ports of Spain, and has ever been the most prosperous. Its inhabitants, the Catalians, were ever "peculiarly jealous of their freedom and their exclusive privileges."

In this library also is a copy of that exceedingly rare book, the polyglot Bible of Cardinal Ximenes. This greatly-celebrated work was produced at Alcalá, not many miles from Madrid, then the seat of the university founded by the cardinal. It should rank as one of the greatest literary achievements of any age, especially when we consider the period in which it was accomplished. Not only was the printing done at Alcalá, but the type was cast there; fifteen years being consumed in the entire labor, and the book finished in 1517.

In Arabic manuscripts the library is somewhat rich; but it might have contained at present literary treasures of inestimable value were it not for the mistaken zeal of this same Ximenes, who destroyed the most precious Arabic manuscripts that fell into the hands of the

Spaniards in their Moorish conquests. After the conquest of Granada, in 1492, he burned thousands of Arabic books and manuscripts, reserving some three hundred only for his university of Alcalá.

Leaving the musty library, where the smiling attendant conveys very plainly that a *real* or two will not come amiss, we seek the Plaza Oriente, near the palace, and walk around its circular garden, admiring the fine equestrian statue of Philip V. in its centre, and the scores of statues surrounding it. These statues are of the heroic size, but not of heroic mould, and are of the kings of Spain, beginning with the very earliest and ending — nobody knows where; for they surround the plaza, are strung all along the walls of the Prado and the park, and stare at one from every nook and corner. It occurs to one, looking at these kingly effigies, that Spain has been very prolific of kings, and has had almost as many as our army has officers. These kings formerly stood around and upon the palace; but it was found that their room was better than their company, and they were thrust out upon the world.

The plazas of Madrid are not numerous, but they have some interest, especially to a Protestant desiring to keep in mind the atrocities of the Romish Church. In the Plaza Verde, for instance, is a cross, marking the spot where the last victim of the Inquisition perished at the stake. As to the *Plaza Mayor* (the Great Square), there formerly took place the atrocious *autos da fé*, when numerous victims were condemned and burned in the presence of the court and distinguished visitors. Should you wish for other proofs than that in the histories, go to the Royal Gallery, and there inquire for a great painting by a contemporary, in which the revolting scenes are depicted with disgusting fidelity.

It was during the regency of the ambitious Cardinal Ximenes that Madrid became the residence of the court, in the early years of the sixteenth century. Through the crazy Joanna, daughter of Ferdinand and Isabella. the crown of Spain came to Charles I., who is also known

FOUNTAIN OF THE SWAN, MADRID.

as Charles V. of Germany. Catalina, another daughter of Ferdinand and Isabella, married Henry VIII. of England, and is known as Catharine of Aragon ; and Isabella herself was descended from a Spanish princess, Constance, daughter of Pedro the Cruel, who had married a prince of England.

But Madrid, from the time of Ximenes, is associated with the royal families of Spain. The growth of Catholic Spain after the death of Ferdinand may be traced in the expansion of Madrid and its influence in affairs. Notwithstanding that Charles I. came into possession of Spain in the plenitude of its power, with all its people united under one government, and with no domestic enemy to fear, yet the decline of Spain commenced with his accession. " He had more power for good or ill in Europe than has been exercised by any man since the reign of Augustus ; and on the whole he did as much harm with it as could possibly be done."

Let us run over the list of rulers since the regency of Cardinal Ximenes, most of whom held their courts at Madrid. Charles I. was born in 1501, king of Spain in 1516, grand duke of Austria in 1519. Nearly all the great discoveries in the New World were made in his reign, for which, however, little thanks the world owes him. In 1555 he abdicated in favor of his son Philip II., the persecutor of heretics, who made Madrid the centre of his work, and who died in 1598. In 1621 Philip III. died. During his reign, in 1609, the last of the Moors were expelled from Spain. Philip IV. died in 1665. The reign of the three Philips is marked by the great decline in the splendid fortunes of Spain. With the Jews and the Moors, whom they had driven out of the country, departed a great measure of the country's prosperity. The Moors, says a writer, had brought to Spain the cultivation of the sugar-cane, cotton, rice, and mulberry. The spices and sweets of Valencia were famous, and so were the blades of Toledo, the silks of Granada, the leather of Cordova. No one knows to-day how much Moorish treasure may yet be buried in Spain. In 1700 Charles II.

8

died; in 1746 died another Philip; in 1759 Ferdinand VI., and in 1788 Charles III., who expelled the Jesuits from Spain, and who was succeeded by Charles IV. In the year 1797 occurred the great naval battle of Cape St. Vincent, and in 1805 the battle of Trafalgar. In 1808 Ferdinand VII. became king, during whose reign the usurper, Joseph Bonaparte, for a brief period was seated upon the throne of Spain. In 1830 was born Isabella, who upon the death of her father, Ferdinand, was proclaimed queen when but two years of age. Trouble began with her birth, and the Carlist plot for the throne. In 1789 Charles IV., grandfather to Ferdinand, had established the succession to the Spanish crown in the female line by "pragmatic sanction," and on the 6th of April, 1830, Ferdinand confirmed this decree. His brother Don Carlos, presumptive heir to the throne, was banished to Portugal in 1832, but incited revolt, in which he was sustained mainly by the Catholics and the mountaineers. He died in 1855; the second Don Carlos, the Count of Montemolin, died in 1861, and the present one is only a nephew of the last.

The Carlists were pretty thoroughly crushed in 1876. Isabella, whose champion was Espartero, married her cousin Don Francisco d'Assisi, in 1841. Her sister married the Duke of Montpensier, fifth son of Louis Philippe, whose palace is in the city of Seville. In 1868 Isabella was expelled from Spain and fled to Paris, where she still resides. In 1870 the crown was offered by the Cortes to Amadeo, son of King Humbert of Italy, and this faint-hearted sovereign abdicated in 1873, when Castellar and others tried to organize Spain as a republic. In 1874 the son of Isabella was made king, under title of Alfonso XII. Alfonso died in 1885, was succeeded by his daughter, Marie de Mercedes; but the present king is the infant born after his death, and known as Alfonso XIII.

Thus skeletonized, we have the history of Spain for the past three hundred years. The people have been mainly true to their rulers, and if any have lost their crowns it has been their own fault. It has been their fault, too, that Madrid is not the attractive city the Spaniards would have it.

There are but few monuments and statues, save those of the ancient kings, which latter seem to have been executed by contract and to have come from the same hand.

Of modern statues that of Cervantes, in front of the House of Deputies, is the best. In the Prado is a monument to commemorate

FOUNTAIN OF THE SEASONS, MADRID.

that horrible act of Murat in 1808, — the massacre of some hundreds of citizens.

Two fine fountains of unique design are prominent in the Prado, which, as the world knows, is the fashionable promenade of Madrid. It is a sight worth the seeing, — the stream of humanity rolling down toward the Prado late in the afternoon, and then streaming back again

early in the evening.   But as it is a well-dressed multitude, and not dis-
tinctive enough to merit more than a glance, we will not stop to describe it.   Only the ragged and dirty, the beggars and gypsies *sui
generis*, are picturesque enough to make us halt for a second glance,
and they pertain mostly to the South.

That we do not attempt a description of the art treasures of the
Museum should rather be placed to our credit, we think, than set down
to any lack of interest in art.   It is, in truth, a stupendous subject, to
undertake to call attention, even, to the treasures of this the finest art
collection of the world.

Did we not wander for hours and hours, through halls and galleries,
and sit in worship before all the painted gods?   To enumerate the
old masters only : there are ten paintings by Raphael, forty-three by
Titian, thirty-four by Tintoretto, forty-six by Murillo, sixty-two by
Rubens, and sixty-four by Velasquez.   It is now sixty years since this
collection was formed, when convents and palaces were made to dis-
gorge their treasures to be placed in the light, and for the enlighten-
ment of the world.

The great centre of Madrid is the *Puerta del Sol* — literally, the
Gate of the Sun — now no gate at all, but the great square of the city
proper, from which diverge the principal streets and avenues.   All the
tramway lines radiate from this point, and the largest hotels are here
situated.   It is certainly a place of the sun, as any one who has to
cross its broad area at midday is painfully aware ; but the heat is
somewhat tempered by an immense fountain in the centre, which
sends forth a great volume of water, with much noise and sparkling of
stream and spray.

That Madrid is a railroad centre, and the centre of art influences
as well, people now concede, in spite of their prejudices.   No one can
call his Spanish tour complete without first visiting or passing through
Madrid.   Still, we do wish Madrid had never been created, and that its
art treasures had been gathered into some old city like Burgos or

Cordova, where their surroundings would form richer settings, historically and architecturally; for they are so alone here, without a suggestion of the time, the circumstance, or the people of the epoch in which the greatest of these paintings were produced. But as lamenting will do no good, what's the use of lamenting? Madrid exists, it is recognized as the nation's capital, and its air seems very well adapted for the preservation of the paintings, as well as for their exhibition.

Finally, we left behind us Madrid with many regrets, — not especially for Madrid, but for the museums and people. We do not pretend to have exhausted Madrid. Edmundo de Amicis was there three months, and left it with the same confession we make, having been there but ten days; but while he devoted so much time to Madrid and then hastily skipped through Cordova and Andalusia, we reversed his plan, — gave all the time we could spare to acquainting ourselves with the true Spain, the España of the poet, the historian, the antiquarian. And we are convinced we did right; for Madrid, interesting though it be to the student of politics, to him who would study the Spain of to-day and the fashions of to-day, has little for him who would acquaint himself with the greater and more glorious Spain of the past. More picturesque people, grander cathedrals and churches, more fascinating vistas of Spain, can be found in any city of Andalusia than in Madrid. Even the bull-fights of Seville are, or ought to be, finer spectacles than those of Madrid; and as to religious processions, those of the North can't "hold a candle" to those of the South.

CHAPTER VII.

TOLEDO, ON THE GOLDEN TAGUS.

ROM Doña Carmen, our amiable landlady of Burgos, we bore a letter to her sister, who eked out a scant income by renting rooms to strangers with good references. Doña Dolores was recently widowed, her husband having suddenly deceased the month previous; so her name of Dolores (the Sorrowful) was applicable. As her maiden name had been, let us say, Gonzales, she was now Doña Dolores Gonzales, *viuda* (or widow) de Garcia. There are many reasons in favor of a woman retaining her maiden name after marriage, the chief being that she is not so completely effaced as with us; and especially should this be a forceful reason if the lady should have acquired a literary or artistic fame previous to marriage. Señorita Smith, for instance, should she happen to marry a man named Brown, would henceforth be addressed as Señora Doña Carlota Smith de Brown, and we would more frequently address her as Doña Smith, or Doña Carlota, than as Mrs. Brown; and the children of the marriage would retain both names until they had (the girls especially) married, and added another to the name of Brown. It is both a means of enlightenment as to their pedigree, and of perplexity to a stranger.

Doña Dolores was gentle, sympathetic, and motherly; her recent grief had plunged her into melancholy but she did not allow it to intrude itself upon her alien household. Besides ourselves there were

A STREET IN TOLEDO.

four boarders, — two bachelors, and a couple newly married, who billed and cooed in a way that seemed to us most obtrusively and unnecessarily affectionate. They were soon to sail for Cuba, and asked us all manner of questions about America and the West Indies, seeming to have some anxiety about the voyage and their reception in a country so far away. They were all tolerable enough, and all very kind, but one of them had some unpleasant habits. As to the table manners of Spaniards in general we feel inclined to say a great deal; but perhaps prudence might suggest silence on this subject.

But it was a pleasant company, and one kindly disposed to the strangers that sat at meat with them twice a day for a week. We soon discovered that the street in which Doña Dolores' house was situated was much out of the way, and it would have been better had we been lodged in the Puerta del Sol, in the centre of the city; but it is a rule with the Club never to move when it can help it, and is at least tolerably situated; and so we stayed there.

Now we will turn to a different subject: One morning early, as the club was taking its "constitutional," walking across the great square of the Puerta del Sol, with the Judge leading the van and the Professor and the Historian bringing up the rear, its ears were assailed by uncommon cries. They proceeded from the newsboys, who had turned out by scores, with their arms full of pamphlets, which proved on inspection to be a new Railway-Guide, — " The Indicador Official de los Caminos de Hierro de España, Portugal, y Mediodia de Francia," full of information for the traveller, but especially rich in new excursion routes, from Paris and Madrid to Barcelona and other parts of Spain. The great fair at Barcelona had set in motion the greater portion of travelling Spain, and the excursion rates had stimulated even the middle classes to indulge in the luxury of a trip to the fine old city on the Mediterranean.

Yet even at greatly reduced and special rates the fares over the Spanish railways are far in advance of our own. Let us quote from our note-book some routes that we jotted down when seeking to include all the principal northern cities in our itinerary. We wished to go to Barcelona, and also include Valencia and Tarragona. The fare direct to Barcelona, second class, *via* Zaragossa, is about 60 *pesetas*, or $12; first class, 80 *pesetas*, or $16: the distance, 700 kilometers, or about 450 miles. By way of Valencia and Tarragona, to return *via* Zaragossa, at least one third farther, excursion tickets were offered at about 90 *pesetas*, or $18. As we also wished to include the Escorial, Burgos, and Zaragossa, we could, by omitting the northern journey to Valencia, go to Burgos from Madrid for 31 *pesetas*, and from Burgos to Barcelona for 44 *pesetas*, or 75 *pesetas* in all, second class, by a roundabout way, with various changes and delays. The rate to Portugal was 96 *pesetas*, straight, and 166 for the excursion. From Madrid to Irun, a distance of 631 kilometers, the fare is, first class, 72 *pesetas* 80 *centimos*, second class 54.60, and third class, 32.80. That is, for 400 miles, first class, the fare is about $15, or nearly 4 cents per mile, and 3 cents second class. We did not wish to go northward, however, as our face was turned toward the south, to Toledo. The trip to Toledo cost less than two dollars, from Madrid; and in this famous old city there is more of real interest (leaving out Madrid's museums) than in the capital itself.

We were constantly saying to ourselves, " To-morrow we will visit Toledo." The Spaniards have a saying: *Mañana* (to-morrow); *siempre mañana* (always to-morrow) ; and to-morrow never comes!

But there was one to-day when we gladly said, This is now, — this is the thing we have so long dreamed of, and now it is realized! Such was the day in Toledo, — the day we first entered it; that city of the Tagus, the golden Tagus, that half encircles it. The river of the poet they call it; because, perhaps, it toils not, nor spins, but simply " roars on forever, Oh, its bosom unvexed by keel of any craft." The city is called one of the oldest in Europe, and no one who has seen it will dare affirm that it is not. Did not the Jews call it

PUERTA DEL SOL, TOLEDO.

Toledoth, the city of their ancestors who forsook Palestine in the time of the great Nebuchadnezzar? It comes into history, at least as early as 193 B. C., when it was taken by the Romans, and then it was large and well populated. After the Romans, the Goths held Toledo, and made it their capital; here reigned King Wamba, and here Roderic, the last king of the Goths, outraged the fair Florinda, whose father, Count Julian, aided the advent of the terrible Moors, and thus avenged himself on his king at the expense of his country's liberty. Some there are, who will tell you there was no fair Florinda, and consequently King Roderic did her no wrong; but we doubt not there was, for have we not seen Florinda's Bath, at the foot of the hill, on the marge of the rich-hued Tagus?

Here, too, we believe, was that scurvy trick played upon old King Wamba, about twelve hundred years ago, whereby he was deprived of his kingdom. He had not wanted the kingdom, in the first place — it was rather forced upon him; but "havings is keepings," and when an usurper wanted to usurp, old Wamba stood in the way. So this usurper, it is said, one Erxigius, gave Wamba a dose of cold poison that plunged the king into a comatose state, by which his attendants thought him about to die. Now no king, in those days, could go straight up to heaven unless he died in the habit of a monk; good Saint Peter wouldn't let him in without the cowl. In all haste, then, they dressed him in the garb of a monk, and when he "came to" — for he didn't die just then, though he has doubtless departed ere this — he was as mad as a hornet; for inasmuch as, according to law, once in the cowl never more a king, old Wamba had to make the best of it and abdicate, living the rest of his life a monk. Sick or well, there was no more royalty for Wamba, and the usurper usurped, opening the way for the dissensions that aided in the downfall of the kingdom; for along came the Moors, in the year 714, captured Toledo, and dwelt therein about three hundred years.

Though the impression Toledo leaves upon the visitor is that of a Gothic city, yet its finest structures, saving the cathedral, are Moorish. The grand old bridge of El Cantara is Romano-Gothic; we cross it in entering the city from the railroad station. Above this bridge, and beyond it, towers the stern old Alcazar, standing on the brow of the hill covered by the houses of the city. Either end is guarded by a massive portal, or tower, and through yet another gateway, called the Puerta del Sol, you enter the city. This is decidedly Moorish, with magnificent horseshoe arches, having those graceful curves that carry one's imagination at once to the Alhambra, to Africa, and the mosques of Cairo.

Below the Puerta del Sol is another gate called the Visagra, standing on the site of an ancient gateway and itself dating from the year 1550. Just inside the main entrance to the city is a curious mosque, said to be at least eight hundred years old, very small, yet showing sixteen Moorish arches, springing from four supporting columns. A Greek cross is painted over the archway, the *escudo* of Alonso VI., who conquered Toledo in 1035, and in the mosque heard the first mass after its capture.

Before entering the city, with its narrow and winding streets, we took a general survey of its surroundings by walking along the encircling *alameda* to a point where the Tagus curves around. It is a pleasant walk outside the wall. To the right, you look down upon the lower terrace, by the river side, where is situated the famous *Fabrica de Armas* (or sword manufactory), the building only a hundred years old; but here are made the " Toledo blades," for which the city has been so long celebrated. It is about the only industry that has survived from ancient times, and it is said that the temper of the swords and sabres made here is still superior. But if one may judge from the samples of jack-knives offered here for sale, the water and the sand of the Tagus have lost some of their virtue.

In a little shop of the town, in a dark and obscure court, we found

BRIDGE OF SAN MARTIN, TOLEDO.

some of the smiths at work on iron jewelry, for which also Toledo has a reputation. They seemed to be worthy and legitimate descendants of Tubal-Cain himself, whose industry and cunning they may have inherited direct, for aught we know to the contrary. They

manufacture a kind of iron jewelry inlaid with gold, which has a
certain beauty of its own, and which they sell at high prices.

Still continuing around the city, beneath the hill on which the main
part of it is built, we come in sight of the noble Bridge of San Martin,
above which, in the river, are the remains of Moorish mills. Below
us are the Baths of Florinda, where, tradition states, the fair daughter
of Count Julian was bathing when King Roderic saw her and became
enamoured of her beauty. Leaving the roaring Tagus behind us, and
entering the gate of the city called the Puerta del Cambron (which
was rebuilt three hundred years ago), we reach that famous convent-
church of San Juan de los Reyes, built by Ferdinand and Isabella,
and consequently nearly four hundred years old. It has the reputation of being one of the finest specimens of florid Gothic art in the
world, as to its interior and its beautiful cloisters. To-day we may
admire what the barbarous French have left us, — the shields, coronets,
and Gothic inscriptions springing about the arches, — and wander
through the beautiful cloisters, with their pointed arches, adorned
with elaborate art. A museum is now shown in one of the cloisters, made up of fragments of statuary, Arabic carvings, and old
paintings.

The most fascinating things about this old convent were on the
outside, in the shape of the chains of captive Christians, hung high
up on the walls. There are hundreds of them, — heavy iron fetters
hung in pairs, votive offerings of the Christians who were delivered
from the Moors at the conquest of Granada. Through four centuries
of change these chains have hung listless against the walls of San
Juan, and their wearers, who came forth so gladly to welcome Ferdinand and Isabella with songs of praise for their deliverance, have
now been dust for near four hundred years.

This was a Christian convent; but up the hill a bit is a memorial
of the Jews, who were formerly so numerous in Toledo. Santa Maria
la Blanca is a Jewish synagogue dating from the twelfth century,

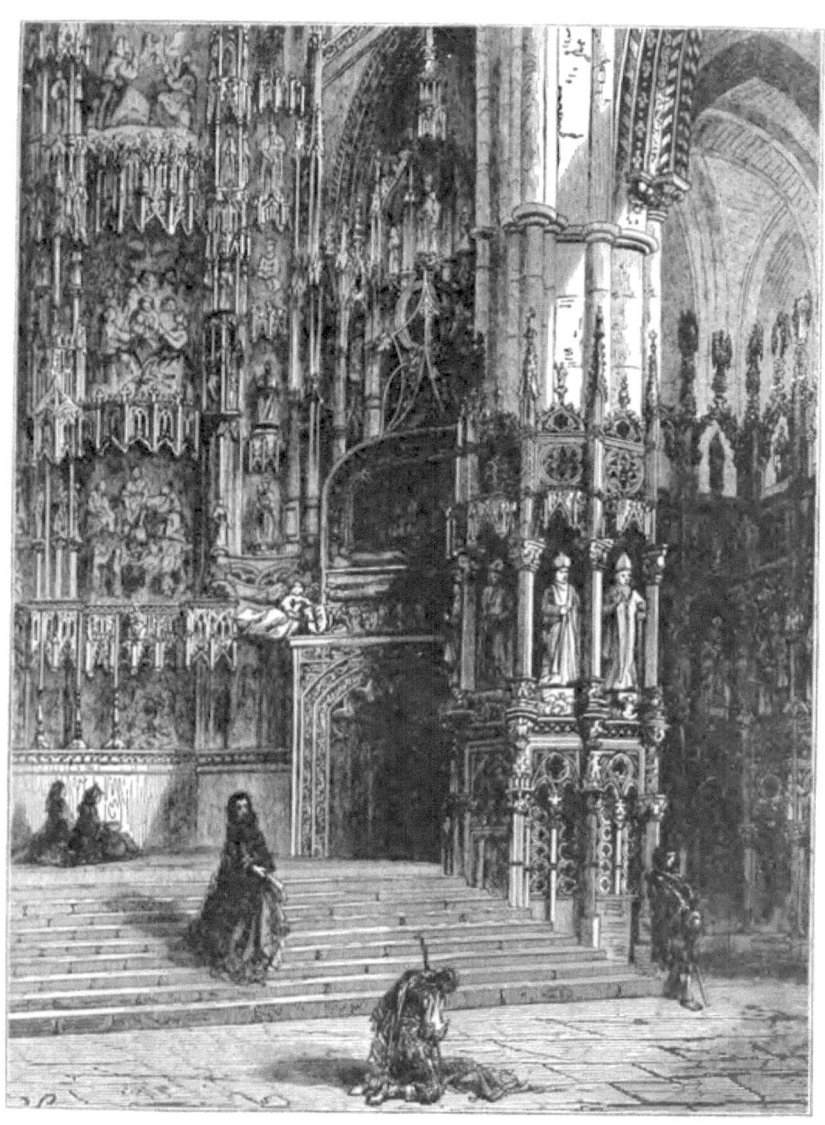

INTERIOR OF THE CATHEDRAL, TOLEDO.

empty now and without any worshippers, but as beautiful as any temple of its size in Toledo. It has the Moorish arches, with polygonal pillars, and a ceiling with beams from the cedars of Lebanon. The earth beneath the pavement is said to have come from Mount Zion; but it is now nearly five hundred years since it was trodden by the foot of a child of Israel.

The Moorish style of architecture prevails, even in these Jewish structures, and also in those called Gothic and Christian; but it may also be seen in its purity in several buildings. As we were climbing one of the narrow streets our guide stopped and knocked at a dilapidated gate. It was opened by a poor woman, who led the way, without a word, to a building used as a carpenter's shop, where the walls were covered with that intricate stucco-work so richly decorative. Time and the smoke of the forge had stained great portions of it, and much had fallen away; but enough remained to show that it was once an important dwelling of the Moors. In this very room, it is said, a Moorish governor cut off the heads of four hundred chiefs of Toledo who had resisted his authority, and whom he invited here to dinner and beheaded as they entered. This place is called El Taller del Moro. Another house we visited, which is preserved in exactly the condition in which the Moors occupied it, with fine inlaid ceiling, with tiled floor, and even draperied in the Moorish manner. This is most interesting, as there are hardly any houses, or even rooms in Spain, that have been preserved as the Moors left them.

Relics of the Goths, the Moors, the Jews, and the so-called Christians are strangely mingled in this quaint old city of Toledo, and it would well repay one a stay of at least a week. Its great cathedral alone needs several days. It is so ancient that they say it was originally erected to the Virgin while she was yet on earth, and she frequently came to see it later on, in company with Saints Peter, Paul, and James. It was converted by the conquering Moors into a mosque.

This was destroyed in the thirteenth century by Saint Ferdinand,
and the present cathedral commenced, which was finished in 1492.
Sculptors and artists from every part were called upon to embellish
it. and it became the most magnificent Gothic structure of its day ;
" it belongs to the pure, vigorous style of the thirteenth century, is
not inferior to any of the great French cathedrals, and far superior
in fine and rich furniture, picturesque effect, and artistic objects of
every kind." The main tower of this cathedral is three hundred
and twenty-five feet high, and terminates in a slender spire encircled
with an imitation of the crown of thorns. The different portals
are rich in sculptures of the fifteenth and sixteenth centuries, and
the bronze doors are most beautiful specimens of their kind.
There are five naves, four hundred feet long, with eighty-four piers
and pillars, and the interior is brightened by painted windows, the
finest as well as the earliest in Spain, some of them dating from
the early years of the fifteenth century. The carvings of the *coro*
are exquisite sculptures in wood, and they have a greater interest for
being faithful representations of incidents in the campaigns of Isabella and Ferdinand, and especially of the siege and capture of the
Alhambra, having been carved in 1495.

The different chapels are worth pages of description, each chapel
having as its centre of attraction some bishop, or king, or saint, famous
in Spain's history from three hundred to six hundred years ago. But
that around which a most peculiar interest attaches is the Capilla
Mozarabe, wherein the Mozarabic ritual is performed daily, — the only
place in Spain where this occurs. The first printed copy of the
Mozarabic ritual, dated 1502, is yet shown to visitors, and reminds
one of the attempt by Spain, in the time of Ximenes, to assert its
independence of Rome. Through the grated door you may see the
painting on the wall of the battle of Oran, in 1514, in which the
great Cardinal Ximenes was directly engaged.

The treasures of the cathedral exceed those of perhaps any other

THE ALCAZAR, TOLEDO.

in Spain; we have not space here to enumerate them. It is said that the French, in 1810, took away two thousand three hundred pounds of silver; but there is a great deal left in plate and shrines and relics. The gold cross crowning a *custodia* of silver weighing ten thousand nine hundred ounces is said to have been made from the first gold brought by Columbus from the New World. Here also is said to be kept the cross of Cardinal Mendoza, which was elevated above the Torre de la Vela at the capture of the Alhambra. and the sword of Alonzo VI., the conqueror of Toledo. Banners are here from the battlefields of Las Navas and Lepanto, and the rich mantle of the Virgin, embroidered with pearls and precious stones.

But who can hope adequately to describe Toledo and its treasures in a single short chapter? Not alone are there treasures in gold and silver, in architecture, painting, and sculpture (chiefly sculptures), but in literature; for in the old library are shown manuscripts of the time of Dante, the works of Saint Gregory, of the thirteenth century, a Talmud, a Koran, a Bible illuminated for Cardinal Ximenes, and a Pliny of the tenth century.

We have described enough, we know, to show that Toledo is well worth travelling long leagues to visit, and deserving of a protracted stay. Unfortunately we could not linger here to breathe in the atmosphere so essential to a finished description. We had to glance here and there, to run to this and ride to that; and though we compassed it all, it was with many a backward, lingering glance that we walked across the bridge of El Cantara, and sought the train that was to carry us to Cordova.

CHAPTER VIII.

DON QUIXOTE'S COUNTRY, AND CORDOVA.

AKING the night train for Cordova, we made a long leap southward, across the provinces of Toledo and Cordova, and over the broad plains of La Mancha. As it was a night-journey little was to be seen of the country till early morning. But just before break of day we reached Manzanares, in the country celebrated as the field of the adventures of that redoubtable knight of Spanish romance, Don Quixote de la Mancha. It is a flat country, with not much to interest the traveller, and one might be pardoned for passing it by without a second glance. Only seven miles distant is the Venta de Quesada, where Quixote was knighted; and not far off the Caves of Montesinos, where the knight had his most wonderful adventures with the enchanted ones. The place where the noble knight did penance is in the sierras, to the left of the Venta de Cardenas, and the veritable windmills with which Don Quixote had his desperate encounter may be seen to the right of the station of Campo de Criptana, on the road to Valencia.

As for Toboso, the home of the peerless Dulcinea del Toboso, is it not well known, and does it not lie fifteen miles from the important station of Alazar de San Juan, also on the route from Madrid to Valencia? Dear old Quixote! For a month past we had been reading ourselves to sleep with his adventures. Every night after

DON QUIXOTE.

lighting the candles and placing them within reach on the stand we popped into bed with the noble "Don" in our hands, and proceeded to follow him and the unctuous Sancho Panza. Several nights we had fallen asleep in the midst of some adventure, only to continue it in our dreams; and to awake with some direful exploit in progress, only to find our candles sputtering, and the *avant-couriers* of dawn struggling into our room. We should like to have seen his adventure with the lions, and to have been present when he set free the galley slaves. We have in our mind's eye yet that "man of goodly aspect, only that his eyes looked at each other," the culprit who was so closely guarded and double-ironed. As for Sancho Panza, with his sturdy figure, his beloved "dapple," and his strings of proverbs, we doubt not we have seen him a dozen times plodding along the dusty roads of the plains, only that we have not been near enough to hear him converse, and so have not benefited by his homely wisdom. It would have been worth the while to see him when tossed in a blanket at the inn, or when he was governor of the island threatening to comb the court doctor's head with a stool.

All the world shares in this interest in Don Quixote; it is said that when the French vandals passed through La Mancha, eighty years ago, they went out of their way a long distance to visit Toboso, and instead of maltreating its inhabitants, as their custom was, fraternized with them, — all on account of Quixote.

Generally bleak and barren, these broad plains in the early days of June are clad in freshest verdure; save that the soil shows thin, and there are few streams to create life when once the sun has dried them up.

We so wanted to wander through Quixote country, and verify the scenes of his adventures, fictitious though they were! But then, we might wander and wander, and so keep on wandering for a year, here in Spain, and then not half exhaust it. And with this we console ourselves, — we will come back next year, perhaps, and gather up those scattered threads of history that have fallen so loosely from our hands.

But we were now approaching Andalusia, the country made famous by the Moors, and Cordova, its chief city during Moorish supremacy. Three hundred years nearly, or until 1030, the Moors ruled in Spain; then their power came to an end, and Moslem Spain was governed by petty kings. Their strifes and rivalries made possible the constant advance southward of the Christian forces, coming down from their mountain fastnesses of Northern Spain.

The last great attempt at universal conquest, operating through Spain, was by the Almohades of Africa, in the year 1212. It took two months to convey this vast army across the straits; but they were met and scattered by Alfonso II. of Castile on the plains of Tolosa. The banner of Alfonso is said to hang in the cathedral of Burgos to-day.

At the station in Cordova we were pounced upon by the omnipresent *cochero*, and taken off to the Fonda Espanola. Though it was very hot, we sallied out without delay in search of the sights of Cordova. Our hotel was on the Calle de Gran Capitan, and the great centre of attraction, the cathedral, was at some distance, through the narrowest and most tortuous streets imaginable. One may "hook it" through Cordova in a day or so by a judicious use of his time; but it is rather a place to linger in, — a city for investigations and prowlings about, with a reasonable expectation of finding a surprise at almost every corner.

And there are many of them, — in truth, Cordova is nearly all corners, like an antiquated donkey; though farther than this the simile does not apply. How we found our way across and around the city is to this day a matter of wonder; perhaps it was our practice in the streets of Burgos, for there we used to lose our way a dozen times a day.

DON QUIXOTE AND SANCHO PANZA.

The cathedral is the great attraction of Cordova; but first we visited the Alcazar, — not, like that of Seville, a magnificent monument of Arabic architecture, but simply a wall-enclosed garden of fine trees, fountains, and flowers. The great walls around it are Roman, to be sure, or Gothic, and massive towers stand up near it with the antiquity of a thousand years upon them. The real building is now used as a prison, and was once occupied by the Inquisition.

The Roman bridge that spans the Guadalquivir just beyond the cathedral is a glorious old structure, with its many arches, and its great square tower on the country side. We went across one morning and photographed it, and also that beautiful bridge. The old mills just beneath it, built by the Moors, may yet be seen grinding the grist of the conquerors of their builders. What the Romans and the Arabs built in Spain they built to last; as witness, their bridges, their mills, and their temples. The Guadalquivir pours over the semicircular dam with tumultuous roar, and winds away toward the hill beyond.

The entrance to the city from the river side is through a large Doric gateway. — the gate of the bridge, — and a little beyond is a queer specimen of a column erected in honor of Saint Rafael, the patron of the city. The guide-books tell us that this old bridge is attributed to Octavius Augustus; its foundations are Roman at least, and it is quite a thousand years old. The bridge and the crumbling towers give one an impression of Cordova's antiquity; but there are churches and convents here that carry one well back to the period when the Moslems were great and flourishing here.

Leaving these minor structures, let us visit the cathedral, — the *mezquita* (or mosque) as it is still called. The time was when Cordova was young, but it was beyond the time of the Romans, for the Carthaginians knew the city as the Gem of the South. It is said that Cæsar destroyed twenty-eight thousand of its population be-

cause it sided with Pompey, and a patrician colony was founded on
its ruins. It became later the capital of the Goths, and still later
of the Arabs. Here flourished literature, art, and science as in no
other part of Europe at that time. The Arabs of Cordova kept
alight the lamp of learning during the dark ages when it was all
but extinguished elsewhere. " The influence of the Spanish Arabs,"
says Prescott, " is discernible, not so much in the amount of knowledge, as in the impulse which they communicated to the long dor-
mant energies of Europe. Their invasion was coeval with the com-
mencement of that long night of darkness which divides the ancient
from the modern world."

It was near the beginning of the caliphate of Cordova that the
great Abderahman conceived the idea of building such a mosque that
all the world would come to wonder at it. Then he sent to all parts
of the Moslem world for columns to adorn his temple; and they came
to him, from not only Moslem countries, but from France, from Seville
and Tarragona in Spain, from Leo the Emperor of Constantinople,
and from the temples of Carthage. As the mosque was built on the
site of a Roman Temple to Janus, doubtless this heathen structure
contributed to the enrichment of its successor. And they may be
seen to-day, — these thousand monoliths of jasper, verde-antique, and
porphyry, a petrified forest of the true Arabian Nights.

There were originally twelve hundred columns, the historians tell
us, but the number now is ten hundred and ninety-six, — enough to
give one visions of vastness, conceptions of grandeur, and ideas of the
infinite. The mosque itself covers four acres; the roof is about forty
feet high, with double arches above the columns, some of them like
interlaced ribbons. There are nineteen longitudinal and thirty-three
transversal aisles, besides several chapels in the laterals, and the great
coro and *capilla mayor* in the centre. What a glorious effect was
produced upon the beholder when all these aisles were open on every
side, and one could look down these vistas of columns, may be faintly

CHAPEL IN THE MOSQUE AT CORDOVA.

realized to-day by standing at the farther end and glancing toward one of the doorways. Beautiful stained-glass windows give a fine effect to other vistas, though it is rather tawdry as compared to the solemn magnificence of the open views. Well may this grand mosque have served as a Mecca for the Spanish Moslems; and it is said to have ranked in sanctity "second only to the famous Kaaba at Mecca."

We cannot express the delight with which we wandered through the mazes of this forest of pillars, looking down the long aisles, peering into the gloomy chapels, the half-ruined Capilla de Villariciosa, the ancient *maksurah*, where were kept the gold and silver vessels of the temple, and the great Koran, which two men could hardly lift. A Gothic inscription, date 1409, may be seen here, also inscriptions in Cufic and African. Beyond is the "holy of holies," or Ceca, the point toward the true Mecca, — East, — where is the exquisitely arched and sculptured *mihrab* (or sanctuary). The *mihrabs* that we examined in Africa, in Algiers, Tlemcen, and Oran, were also beautiful; but this excels them all, with its interlaced arches and beautiful mosaics. These latter are said to be Roman-Byzantine, and were sent by the Emperor Leo, of Constantinople, in the year 965, accompanied by a Greek, who taught the Moors the art. A celebrated Koran in illuminated manuscript was treasured here; but when the city was taken by Alonzo it was torn in pieces by the soldiery.

Some three hundred and sixty years ago the Spaniards made an "improvement" in the mosque by introducing the large *coro* — a church in itself— into the centre. Though beautiful in its way, with its brass balustrades and carven-seated *silleria*, yet as Charles V. (so often quoted) is *said* to have said: "It is only what might have been built anywhere else, but they destroyed what was antique in the world."

Fortunately for us, at the time of our visit a feast-day occurred, — just what it was we don't know, nor care, for every day in the calendar has its saint, and every saint its feast-day; but, brought out from their concealment, rich tapestries were hung upon the walls of the opposite church, and an altar erected in the street, with a fine painting and a good one, behind it.

About six o'clock the procession was formed; people flocked

VALENCIAN LABORER.

hither from all quarters of the city, and the streets were crowded. Foreseeing this state of things, we climbed the belfry-tower and gazed down calmly upon the multitudes beneath. Flocks of boys in white gowns and priests in petticoats gathered about the doors of the cathedral, and soon they began to fetch out their candlesticks and holy images, — brass and silver and gilt. Every boy carried a candle. Then there were troops of girls, — hundreds of them. They stretched half around the great mosque, and the line of images was unbroken for a long distance.

A band was in attendance and played a lovely air, but soon the music died away, and the noise of shuffling feet ceased about the time the sun went down; the shadow of the tower that had crept slowly

INTERIOR OF THE MOSQUE AT CORDOVA.

across the roof-tops across the river and out over the plain beyond now lost itself in the gathering gloom of night. Yet we lingered, looking again and again over this quaint old city, loath to leave it to itself. Beyond the roofs of tiles, here and there stood up the massive towers of Goths and Romans, rich-hued and time-defying; cool and dark rose the near Sierra, with its terraced gardens, its hermitages, and its *vales paraisos* (or vales of paradise); while clear-cut against the distant sky stood out the castle of Almodoxar, eight miles away.

Beneath us lay the court of oranges, the grand entrance-plaza to the mosque, its ranks of orange-trees so planned as to be a continuation of the lines of columns within the temple, and its fountain to refresh all true believers. A few palms rise above the orange-trees, but they are wind-torn and scraggy; yet they remind the student of history of their introduction here by Abderahman more than eleven hundred years ago. "Beautiful palm, thou art, like me, a stranger here; but the western breezes kiss thy branches, thy roots strike into fertile soil, and thy head rises into a pure sky."

A curious type of a Spaniard, says the Baron Ch. D'Avillier, in his work on Spain, is the *baratero*, who is a man from the dregs of the people, but who is dangerously expert in handling the knife, and who trades upon the terror he inspires, by exacting blackmail from fortunate gamesters. Each town has a certain number of men of no profession, called *tahures* (or gamblers), whose industry is play. The edicts of Alphonso the Wise against *tahurerias* (or gambling-houses) serve to show that during his time the love of play was sufficiently strong to warrant State interference; and if we are to believe the testimony of a Sevillian author, Fajardo, the vice was still as deeply rooted toward the end of the seventeenth century. This author gives an account of the tricks practised by the swindlers in the pay of the *grecs* of the period. To-day the player of Spain has less faith in chance than in the address of his fingers. The *garitos* are not the only resorts of gamblers; they meet everywhere, — on the shore, under the shade of a boat, beneath the umbrageous trees, or under an old wall in some obscure corner. The parties are made up of vagrants, to whom are added soldiers or sailors. They play *pecao* or *cané;* their faces are agitated and unquiet-looking, affected either by the passion of play or by fear of seeing an *alguacil* arrive. Suddenly, without knowing whence he came, a man of pale complexion, wearing a sinister expression of face, and a bold insulting aspect, appears in the midst of the group. He has a robust frame, and carries his jacket over his broad shoulder, while his short trousers are held up by a wide silk waistband. He is a *baratero*, who has thus unceremoniously installed himself among the players, and who calmly announces that he has come to deduct his share of the profits. The amount of this blackmail is usually small, — about ten centimes to the game.

"*Ahí va eso!*" cried the *baratero*, casting down into the middle of the group something done up in a dirty piece of paper, which had probably served to wrap up fried fish. It was a packet of cards, — *baraja,* that is. "What does it signify if you play with these cards? Here no one dare play, but with my cards." If the players are inclined to submit, the *baratero* pockets his *cuartos*, and the play passes off quietly. But it sometimes happens that in the group there is an awkward character to deal with, a *valiente*, — valiant man, literally, — a *mozo cruo* (an almost untranslatable Andalusian expression, which denotes a youth endowed with the attributes of pluck, hardihood, and pride), who would fearlessly reply, "*Camarà, nojotros no necesitamos jeso!*" ("Comrade, we have no need of them!") as he hands back the cards to the *baratero;* who replies, "*Chiquiyo, venga aquí el barato y sonsoniche!*" ("Boy, make haste and hand me the *barato:* not another word!") The *mozo cruo* then draws a long knife from his vest, and opening it with a clang of its spring, drives the point close to the stakes, and exclaims, while he glares defiance at the

A BARATERO.

intruder, " *Aqui no se cobra el barato sino con la punta de una navaja* " (" Here the *barato* is only reached by the point of the *navaja* "). The challenge is usually accepted, and the adversaries pronounce the solemn " *Vamonos !* " or " *Vamos alli !* " (" Let us go! ") or, " *Vamos á echar un viaje!* " (" Let us make a journey! ") It is their *jacta est alea.* Then repairing to some retired spot, the *navajas* or *puñals* are drawn, gleam for an instant in the light, and one of the combatants is sacrificed. But crimes of this sort do not always remain unpunished : it sometimes happens that two or three months later one hears in the streets of the town the sound of a small bell, and the voice of a man asking alms *para decir misas por el alma de un pobre que van á ajusticar* (" to say masses for the soul of an unfortunate man who is about to be executed ").

At other times two *barateros* meet on the same ground, and either agree to divide their share of the stakes, or to fight a duel, which is certain to terminate fatally to one of them ; or it may be that the *baratero* who surprises a group of players is merely a blustering bully, who is only audacious with the timid, and skulks off when he encounters a formidable foe, — a type known by the name of *maton*, the *matachin*, the *valenton*, the *perdonavidas*, etc. When two braves of this sort meet, a most amusing dialogue takes place between them, of which we will try to give some notion, although the Andalusian language loses greatly by translation into another tongue.

" *Ea !* it is here that the braves are about to perform," cries one of them, as he makes the spring of his *navaja* ring.

" *Tire osté !* Draw, comrade Juan," cries the other as he walks round his adversary.

" *Vente á mi, Curriyo !* Not so much skulking around."

" It is you, *zeño* Juan, who leap like a little dog."

" *Ea, Dios mio !* Hold, while you commend your soul to God! "

" Have I wounded you ? "

" No, it is nothing."

" Ah ! well, I mean to slay you with a blow. You may ask for extreme unction."

" Escape, *por Dios, Curriyo!* You see you are in my power, and I mean to bore a hole in you larger than the arch of yonder bridge."

This dialogue would last for more than an hour if the friends did not interpose ; and the two adversaries, who are ready to be appeased, close their knives and adjourn to some *taberna*, where their wrath is drowned in a *canez de jarez.*

One can almost foretell the end of the *baratero :* it is on the scaffold, erected in some public place to carry out the punishment of the *garrote.*

The days were hot, tropical, intense, but the nights were cool. At mid-day little life was stirring ; but towards five o'clock the people came pouring out of their houses in swarms, and filled the streets and plazas. The noise of their assembling, the roar of voices, lasted well toward midnight ; at sunset, when the Sierra was crowned with great crimson banks of clouds, the squares were filled with multitudes, sitting at tables sipping drinks and ices, and promenading the central walks. We regretted that we could not stay another week in ancient Cordova, it was so quaint and cleanly, and the halo of history came so near to earth.

CHAPTER IX.

N a study of the Arabs in Spain, the two cities of Seville and Cordova should be grouped together, for they were interdependent, and the fall of the first but hastened that of the other. We wanted to linger a longer time in Cordova; but the world moves on and on, and one can't stay always in one spot. So we ventured on once more.

Until two o'clock that afternoon we travelled southeast into the heart of the Province of Sevilla. It was a pleasant country, undulating at first, then more level, with fields of wheat and barley stretching as far as the eye could reach, with hills and knolls covered with olive-trees and broad stretches of vineyards.

The first day of our arrival we saw little of Seville, because we did not arrive until well into the night; the second day was the Sabbath. But we anticipate. Seville was full and running over; for all the world (immediately contiguous to the district) was there, and all the world seemed to have taken with it wife and children. Hotels were filled, boarding-houses likewise, and the hackmen were more impudent than usual; for a hackman, be it known, rises and falls in barometric scale with the influx and departure of strangers. Double rates were sanctioned by the authorities, and double rates were charged. Fortunately there were but two vacant rooms at the Spanish hotel, El Cisne and Nueva York (the Swan and New York). Just why a hotel of

pretensions should saddle itself with such a name as this our readers
know as well as we.

The great fair was the theme of every scribbler for weeks.   It had
attracted, as we have said, the attention of all natives and strangers.
Just outside the city walls, not far from the banks of the Guadalquivir,
hundreds of booths and shanties had been erected for the accommoda-

ON THE WAY TO THE FAIR.

tion of the venders of many articles, and for the temporary sojourn
of the families of the Sevillanos, especially in the afternoon and evening.   And the city fathers had outdone all previous efforts — for this
fair is an annual occurrence — in providing entertainment for the
crowds.   They had barely recovered from the *Solemnidades* of Holy
Week, which took place between March 25 and April 2 ; after allow-

ing themselves a week to breathe in, they sprang to their second task with renewed ardor. Easter Sunday was particularly "solemn and beautiful," to judge from the official announcement at the time. In the morning the city officials waited upon the archbishop at his palace, to conduct him to the cathedral for high mass, and in the afternoon they all skipped off to a "grand and solemn bull-fight!" The official announcement reads somewhat like the advertisements of the "sacred" concerts that take place in the theatres of American cities of a Sunday: "In the evening of April 1, Day of the Resurrection, will be celebrated a grand bull-fight, with bulls from the renowned *hacienda* of Don Diego Benjumea, and with the celebrated swordsmen, Frascuelo, Mazzantini, and Espartero, as fighters. At night, the spring season will be inaugurated in the theatre San Fernando."

Well, after this they took a needed rest until the 15th of April, when the fair was publicly opened by a bull-fight. This Sunday bull-fight was announced as something especially fine, inasmuch as the bulls were to come from the *hacienda* of the Excellentissimo Señor Don José Orozco, and were expected to die game only after ripping up numerous horses, putting the picadors to the peril of their lives, and furnishing fun for the million. Other bull-fights were announced for the week, but all were urged to patronize that of the Sunday, as our citizens are urged to attend the "sacred" concerts and minstrel-shows, for the recreation it would give them. On Monday, there was to be a distribution of bread to the poor, with *fuegos artificiales* (or fire-works) at night. On Tuesday, grand competitive *concurso* of bands of music, with fifteen hundred *pesetas* as first prize, eight hundred for the second, and honorable mention for the third. On Wednesday, *gran corrida de toros* (bull-fight), in which eight bulls were to be slain, and four *espadas* to take part, — Frascuelo, Mazzantini, Espartero, and Guerrero; also elevation of *fantoches* and *fuegos artificiales*. On Thursday, another bull-fight, another elevation of *fantoches*, more fire-works; also another sacrifice of eight bulls. On Friday, *otro gran corrida de toros* (another

bull-fight), with eight bulls from the *ganaeria* of the Excellentissima
Señora Marquesa Vinda del Saltillo. As the excellent Marquesa was
a widow and a woman, every man with a spark of gallantry was
expected to attend. Report says that the widow's bulls fought well,
and did not cause the blush of shame to mantle her fair cheek.

Anent these bull-fights, an acquaintance told us the following
story: A Spanish friend of his came to his door one night, late, and
after gaining entrance, threw himself upon the bed, with sobs and
cries. For a long time he lay there overpowered by some bitter grief.
At last he said in broken tones: " My sister — dead. I must go
to the funeral." He refused to be comforted. " She is dead — and
that is not all. I must go to the funeral; and if I go to the funeral
I can't go to the bull-fight! Oh, my sister! my sister! Oh, why did
you die at this time! My sister — the bull-fight. To think, — eight
bulls, four *espadas!* Oh, my sister — the bull-fight! Alas! why did you
die at this time! I am most miserable — my sister — the *toros!*
Never shall I see them again!"

To a stranger, this fair, this assembling together of thousands
of natives, especially such a concourse of the *paisanos* (or country
people), could not fail of being interesting and instructive. As we
were walking one morning along the *paseo* on the banks of the
Guadalquivir we heard a confused tinkling of bells and shouts.
Bearing down upon us was a vast flock of Merino sheep, large-
formed, shaggy-coated, filling the road for a long distance, guided
by gaunt shepherds in sheepskin, with long pikes, and their provision
laden upon a diminutive donkey.

At another turn we were nearly run over by a galloping drove
of bulls and oxen, which came tearing down a cross avenue, followed
and headed by several wild-looking *vaqueros* on scrawny steeds, and
brandishing pikestaffs like lances. An immense drove of hogs came
next, and then more sheep, more cattle, droves of horses, troops of
donkeys, the latter always heavily laden with panniers full of young-

HALL OF THE AMBASSADORS, SEVILLE.

sters and women, astride or riding sideways, crab-fashion. And so they came in — thousands of animals, four-legged and two-legged — and camped in the open place set apart between the great tobacco factory, the garden of the Duke Montpensier, and the walls of the ancient city. At night their camp-fires were lighted, they sang and danced, and extorted doubtful music from primitive instruments.

Every afternoon the *paseos* are crowded with visitors, poor and rich, high and low. In every booth the Andalusian dance went on, attracting crowds of observers at the doors. Such a number of fair sweet faces and mischievous black eyes it would be difficult to find assembled again — until the time comes for another fair.

Not the least interesting places were the side-shows, which were wonderfully like those at our own fairs and cattle-shows. Thus there was the *Gran Vista del Mundo* (the Greatest Collection of Marvels on Earth), the headless woman, the Sphinx, the *Museo Anatómico*, etc. Standing in front of these were dirty and ragged showmen, loud of mouth, scant of modesty, and as impudent as Barnum himself. It was a vast crowd, but it was a very good-natured one. We mingled with it every day in the week, saw hundreds, yes thousands, of men drinking, and engaged in friendly altercation, but did not see one man really intoxicated.

Towards the end of the week the crowd of countrymen began to melt away; tents were pulled up, and the flocks and herds started on their journey over the dusty roads; and on Saturday when we took our morning walk to the fair grounds there was but a small portion of them left. We missed them very much, for in the morning, later on, there were but few people out in the gardens and along the river.

A bridge, a fine stone and iron structure, spans the Guadalquivir River, about half a mile distant from the centre of the city. The bull-ring lies about half-way between these two, fronting the river. Close to this, on the bank, stands the Tower of Gold (*Torre del Oro*).

We had always thought this tower was so called because of the color of its porcelain dome, but believe now it derived its name from the fact that gold had been stored there in olden times.

The grand *paseo* of Seville really begins about here, and also a system of gardens that run along and near the left bank of the Guadalquivir for more than a mile. Most fragrant and delicious are these gardens of roses and orange-trees, where song-thrushes warble night and day. Banks and bowers of roses perfume the air, and the nearly-opened orange-buds scent every breeze. It was our custom to ramble out through the city gate every morning, in the direction of the gardens, halting at a building in the centre of one of them to take our morning coffee.

This building, which had been erected as a summer theatre, was of a light and graceful structure, with open sides, a handsome stage and scenery. As we would sit there sipping our coffee, the balmy breezes, incense-laden, would come drifting in, and the birds in the laurel-trees made musical the morning hours. In the evening — for such was the fascination of this place that we frequently went out there after dark — the garden was enlivened by delightful music from the violins, guitars, and tambourines of an excellent band of *estudiantes*, — true Spanish students, — with graceful cloak, cocked hat, and wooden spoon.

We are now ready to enter the country containing the richest remains of Moorish cities; for while the Goths bestowed upon Spain the rich gift of expressive idioms, the architecture fittest to survive is that only of the Moors. Seville under the Moors was a seat of learning, and a centre of silk manufacture. The Moors held it five hundred years, surrendering to King Ferdinand I. in December, 1248. What those five hundred years of Moorish possession brought forth, we see to-day in the architectural remains, the finest of Seville.

But we are in danger of side-tracking ourselves in these reflections; the broad road of Spanish history lay shining before us, yet we

THE GIRALDA, SEVILLE.

wander off into a by-path. For this lapse let us now make amends. We had intended to describe the sights of Seville, the city lying in the curve of the Guadalquivir. Its streets are so crooked that one finds difficulty in going to any place at all; in fact, you cannot go straight, for every hundred yards there is a turning or a corner.

We had started out many times, with the fixed determination of visiting a certain spot, and had as many times returned without reaching it. At last, in despair of knowing the city in any other way, we went up into the tower of the Giralda, with a map, and then descended and made the entire circuit of Seville. You know, of course, that the Giralda is the lion of Seville, sharing its honors with the Alcazar. Perhaps we need not repeat that it was built by the Moors, at the command of Abu Yacub, in the year 1196. It was a good enough tower as it was, and two hundred and fifty feet in height, but the Spaniards added another belfry in 1568, making it one hundred feet higher. The original shape of the tower was that of the great minarets of Africa, such as are in Tlemcen and Tangiers. That the Spaniards improved it must be open to doubt; but the crowning abomination is that bronze figure of Faith, called the " Girandillo," with its great flapper, supposed to represent the banner of Constantine. It is visible from afar off, and at a distance looks like a great pouter pigeon ; a nearer view gives the banner the appearance of the broad leaf of an old-fashioned tea-table. Wherever you may go in the city and its vicinity this inconstant Faith (for it is a weathercock) may always be seen, and as it rises at the end of some narrow street, ever attracts the attention. It seems a part of the great cathedral itself, as it is, indeed, its belfry; for the ancient Spaniards were not averse to making useful the public works as well as the houses of the Moors. A mumbling of prayers, a dash of holy water, and a little whitewash, and presto! the Moorish minaret was the belfry of the Christian church, and the mosque, served in a like manner, the church itself. As in ancient times the Muezzins sum-

moned the faithful to prayer and repose, so now the jangling of many
bells serves a like purpose for the so-called Christians.

It matters not to us, Catholic or Mohammedan, so we may climb
the tower and feast our eyes upon the prospect spread below. You
ascend (after paying the portress two *reals*), by a series of ramps of
very easy incline, to the top of the great tower, where the bells are
hung ; these bells are named after the apostles, we believe, and are
of every shape and size and tone. Just before sunset is the best
time for the ascent; we know, because we have tried it at all hours.
Immediately beneath you is the cathedral, with its vast gray domes,
its hundreds of flying buttresses, its towers and pinnacles, looking
like an unfinished dwelling of the Cyclops. Troops of swallows
skim the air at this hour, and scores of sparrow-hawks pounce down
from their lairs in tower and belfry. Beneath, again, is the *patio* of
orange-trees, around which are the priest's quarters, and structures
dependent upon the cathedral.

The fragrance of orange-blossoms sometimes reaches to this height,
as well as does the din from the streets. An ancient city like this,
with all its structures of imperishable stone, with roofs, tiles, and
narrow streets, presents somewhat the appearance of a vast rocky
plain with hillocks and rocky mounts and innumerable rivulets
wandering through, which have worn deep channels in them, like
miniature Colorado cañons. These rivulets are the streets, overhung
by high houses, and which pour forth floods of humanity, — hundreds
of men and women, boys and girls, crazily flitting about, consuming
the precious moments of their worthless lives.

Being elevated far above our fellow-mortals, we can look down
upon them with calm contempt, — as we do, improving this opportunity for reflections upon their follies. But the hives of these insects
are far more interesting than they, and there they lie before us, ·
an agglomeration of stone cells, stretching away and away, with the
river bounding them on two sides, and on two others the verdant plain.

INTERIOR OF THE CATHEDRAL, SEVILLE.

The walls of Seville, it is said, are more than a league in circuit; but you might walk around for hours without seeing a wall, so much have they been incorporated into the city itself. In our morning walk we did, finally, find some noble ruins of great walls with towers and gates, — massive, time-defying, but altogether useless. Some of the city gates are worth studying to-day, and all of the *plazas* are worth visiting. Looking down upon the sea of roofs, nearly every house seems covered with a garden; for the guttered tiles have retained moisture and silt enough to give attachment to millions of plants, and these were in full bloom, so that masses of greens and yellows mingled with the rich reds of the tiles.

The *plazas* appear merely as small openings in this stone city. Nearest to the tower is the *Plaza del Triunfo* (or Place of Triumph), bounded by the Cathedral, the Alcazar, and the Lonja. In the far end of the city is a neglected *plaza* containing the famous statues of Hercules, of Roman origin, yet retaining strength and beauty, though corroded by the elements through many centuries.

The *plazas* are breathing-places only, and do not offer that freedom and enjoyment of the gardens of Delicias, and the *paseos* along the Guadalquivir. Few trees grow in them; their stone benches are cold at evening and exposed to the sun during the day, and the stranger in the city is not likely to fall in love with the *plazas*.

The sun, which all day has blazed away his fiercest rays at the city, is now sinking rapidly toward the hills beyond the Guadalquivir, his store of ammunition exhausted, and bestowing upon us the blessed period of the twilight; levelled rays glance from roof to roof, half an orb only peers above the horizon, and lengthened shadows stretch along the plain. At last he is out of sight; only the banks of crimson clouds with golden borders betray his recent exit. A grateful coolness pervades the air, and now the multitudes pour forth into the streets and *plazas* to enjoy the evening out of doors.

Cool and dark, by day as well as by night, is the great cathedral, with its treasure dimly visible in the soft light that streams through the ninety beautiful windows. To describe these treasures of art and history would need more time and more space than are now at my disposal. Suffice it to enumerate some of the things that attract the crowds of tourists hither. Should you enter by the doorway at the foot of the tower you might notice the wooden effigy of a crocodile hung in chains far overhead, and an elephant tusk, — presents, these, from the grand Soldan of Africa some six centuries ago. Immediately in front and behind the high altar is the *Capilla Real* (the Royal Chapel), containing the remains of Saint Ferdinand in a shrine of bronze and silver, crystal and gold. The banner and sword, and an image of the Virgin which this conqueror of Andalusia carried at his saddle-bow, are also shown.

Beyond is the Sacristia Mayor, with precious paintings by Murillo and Pedro Campana, the immense silver *custodia* (or silver temple), four stories high, *el tenebrario* (the great bronze candlestick), twenty-five feet high, and other treasures. The chapels, with fine marbles and paintings, are numerous on every side; perhaps that containing Murillo's famous vision of San Antonio is the most sought after. The high altar, the choir, the exquisitely sculptured organs, — all these claim the attention; but that which oftenest drew us to the cathedral was the marble slab above the remains of Fernando Columbus, — the same marble that once covered the ashes of Columbus. The dead discoverer was first placed to rest in the Convent of St. Francis, at Valladolid; but six years later he was removed to the Carthusian monastery at Seville, where a costly monument was raised over his remains by Ferdinand, with the inscription: " A Castilla y Leon, Mundo Nuevo dió Colon."

The most interesting of all Seville's attractions is, of course, that palace of the ancient Moors, — the Alcazar. It not only retains the name but the pronunciation of the Arabs; for, departing from established rules, the Spaniards speak of it as the Alcázar instead of

MOORISH ARCHES OF THE ALCAZAR, SEVILLE.

the Alcazár. This beautiful palace we almost despair of describing
to our readers. Nearly all of the seventy-eight apartments are rich
in mosaics and fanciful arabesques. Only a detailed description
(which present space at our disposal forbids) can convey an adequate
idea of its beauty. The great central Patio of the Princesses, they
tell us, was so called because here were gathered the beautiful
maidens, one hundred in number, sent as annual tribute to the
Moorish king. The most glorious hall is that of the Ambassadors,
with its lofty " half-orange " ceiling of golden honeycomb work.

Beautiful as it is, the Alcazar has a superior in the Alhambra,
which has a great advantage from its position alone. No garden
that we have yet seen, however, can vie with that attached to the
Alcazar, with its fantastic forms of shrub and tree, its delicious
orange and laurel hedges, its kiosks, fountains, fish-ponds, and fragrant flowers. Rich in reminiscences of royalty are the Alcazar
and the garden : of kings, and Spanish, from Masa the Moor to
Pedro the Cruel, Charles V., and the disgusting Philips ; not to
speak of such as, in our own time, paraded their follies before the
world. A great wall surrounds both garden and palace, and, as
with the Alhambra, the visitor has no suspicion of so much magnificence until he has passed the portals.

A more modern palace, copied after the architecture of the Moors,
is that called the Casa de Pilatos, because said to be built in imitation of the house of Pilate, in Jerusalem. In tile mosaic it has no
equal, perhaps, except in the Alcazar and the Alhambra, and the
visitor walks in wonder through its marvellous halls and corridors.

Of churches and convents Seville possesses more than enough,
even though many have been destroyed by the vandal French and
suppressed by government. One should see San Lorenzo, with its
fine paintings, the splendid roof of San Clemento, San Pablo, and
San Pedro with its Moorish tower ; also San Isadora, and Santa
Maria Blanca. In the *Caridad* (or charity hospital), or rather in

the church attached, are several Murillos, among them his finest
works: "The Loaves and Fishes," "Moses striking the Rock," and
a "Saint John of God." The last seems to be the best picture by
this artist, — the best small picture we have seen.   ·

To see Murillos in numbers, without respect to their merit, one
should visit the Museo, where are twenty or thirty by the great master, as well as others by painters of great fame in Spain. This collection is carefully catalogued and arranged for intelligent study.
The building itself containing the paintings is very fine ; and the
side saloons and obscure galleries are full of paintings of great
merit, which are doomed to obscurity because of the super-excellence
of the greater works.

Perhaps our readers would like to go with us to the bull-ring,
and there witness, through our eyes, that national pastime. It is a
brutal spectacle, we must admit, and a survival of the gladiatorial
combats of the ancient Romans. But, assuming that we did not
go there *de gusto* (or from choice), but out of a sense of duty as it
were, we will proceed to describe what we saw. One day as we
meandered down the street during the week of the fair we found
our progress barred by a crowd, every male member of which had
his hat in his hand ; for a long procession was passing, bearing in
its midst the most holy *custodia* and other relics from the cathedral. The long street was entirely canopied, and the balconies on
either side filled with gay and beautiful *señoras* and *señoritas*, shield-
ing their eyes from the sun by means of parasols and fans. This
procession paraded the principal streets and then disappeared beneath
the lofty domes of the cathedral. We followed the crowd, of course,
and learned that the greater portion of them were going, in the afternoon, to the bull-fight.

The Judge remarked that this was our opportunity. Our Spanish
education would not be complete without a glimpse at least of the
national sport ; so it was resolved that the Judge should purchase our

THE PICADOR.

party some tickets in the *sombra*, which he did, and at the proper
time all were assembled at the gate of the great building. A dense
crowd was fighting for admittance, although it was an hour before
the performance was to begin, and we had to struggle hard to secure
our seats. But it was a good-natured crowd mainly, and when we
were once inside we had no difficulty in selecting our places; then
we turned to watch the thousands of others now pouring into the
great amphitheatre. The bull-ring is surrounded on all sides by a
barrier some five feet high, back of which is a narrow space, and above
this rise the terraces of stone seats, tier above tier, the topmost surmounted by a roofed corridor. The best seats are in the shade;
the great amphitheatre is divided into *sol* and *sombra* (or sun and
shade), those in the shade being twice the price of those in the sun.
As the sunny side is very hot and glaring, all those who could,
bought seats in the shade; even the ragged beggars, whose filth and
misery were almost impossible to imagine, fought hard to get seats
where the heat was not too intense. At last the hour approached.
In a great box in the upper row, canopied and adorned with flags,
sat the *presidente* (the master of ceremonies), surrounded by his friends.
At a given signal a gate was thrown open, and 'in pranced the *alcalde*
(or master of the ring), who put his spirited horse through a variety
of evolutions that quite captivated the crowd. He advanced to a
point beneath the president's box, and begged of him the key, assur-
ing him that if he would grant that favor he would let in one of the
most magnificent bulls in the world. The key was tossed to him,
and he galloped back to the opposite side of the arena, and then
entered the bull-fighters; the *capeadores*, or those who were to swing
the *capas* (or colored scarfs), to attract the attention of the bull away
from a fallen *picador* (or mounted spearman); there followed next the
picadores mounted on poor old horses, destined to be killed; next
came the *banderilleros*, or the men who planted the barbed darts
in the shoulders of the bulls to infuriate them. At the head of

THE ESPADA.

this procession marched the *espadas* (or swordsmen), the principal
actors in the bloody scene, and at the rear came the minor personages, who waited upon the others. All were gayly dressed, the *picadores* with embroidered jackets and silver-mounted saddles, and the
espadas most resplendent in gold and silver embroidery. These last
were well known; each one carried himself with the air of a prince,
and each one wore a little pug (or *chignon*) at the back of his head.
The pictures will present all these peculiar features, and are almost
self-explanatory, so we will not waste further time describing what is
not necessary.

They took their various positions, and then the gate was thrown
open and in charged the first bull. He came in at a tremendous
rate, but halted in the centre, pawed the ground a little, and then
rushed directly upon the nearest horse, planted his horns in its
breast, and next moment that poor beast was lying on the sand
dying, the blood gushing out in a torrent. The *picador* was hardly

prepared for this quick onslaught, and was tumbled from his saddle and pinned by one leg to the ground, while the bull madly and repeatedly gored the dying horse. Several *capeadores* rushed to the rescue, flaunting their *capas* in the face of the bull, and succeeded in diverting his attention to themselves while the bruised *picador* was extricated and led limping away beyond the barrier. The bull's blood was up, and he charged upon and tore up the sides of another poor

PLAY OF THE CAPE.

horse, which galloped half around the ring before it fell. Then another was served in the same way, and all was confusion; the *capeadores* striving to aid the fallen spearmen, and look out for themselves at the same time, while the bull charged upon this person and that in succession.

As for the spectators, they nearly went wild with enthusiasm, clapped their hands, pounded with their canes, and shouted, " Bravo toro!" till they were hoarse. As though the bull were not mad

enough, and had not proved himself brave enough already, he was
to be further tormented by the *banderillero*, who took his stand in the
ring and tempted the *toro* to charge. The bull charged him, and as
he approached and lowered his horns, the man (or fiend) planted
a barbed dart in either shoulder, and then dexterously leaped aside.
Two other pairs were planted in the same manner, until the bull was
furious, and bellowing from the pain. Then the other fighters all
retired, and the arena was left to the bull. A trumpet was sounded,
and into the arena leaped the swordsman, and gayly advanced to
meet the bull, with his scarlet *capa* over his left shoulder, and a
sharp sword extended in his right hand. The spectators held their
breath as bull and man advanced to meet each other. The bull lowered his horns to charge, and then out flashed that glittering sword,
and *toro* lay dying on the sands.

There! That is a brief description of the bull-fight; only it is
much more barbarous, perhaps, than we have represented it. No bull
ever leaves the ring alive; he is driven in to be slain. Each bull is
expected to kill two or three horses; and it is this feature of the
spectacle that is the most revolting, for the poor horses are stood up
defenceless to be slaughtered, and they are not always immediately
killed, but are most shockingly lacerated. Sometimes, if they survive
a fight, they are taken out, their gaping wounds sewn up, and used
again. Like the bulls, they must be eventually killed. Six or eight
bulls and from fifteen to twenty horses are slain in the average bull-
fight. Each scene with each bull is but a repetition of that described,
with slight variations. Just as soon as the bull is killed, a team of
gayly-decorated mules is driven in, the bull drawn out by his horns
and the horses by their necks, the gates again closed, sand swept over
the pools of gore, and another bull driven in to share the fate of his
companions. The second bull was not so " game " as the first, and
wounded but two horses; the third was a large brindled bull, which
wounded three; the fourth was a coward, which was played with by

THE CACHETERO.

a lasso-thrower (after the Mexican style); the fifth was "tailed," — thrown to the ground by a sharp jerk of his tail; the sixth killed one horse and wounded another, and the crowd clamoring for his death and the *espada* failing to kill him, the butcher was called in, who "stuck" him with a short sharp knife behind the horns; the seventh was very game, and would not die, though stuck by the swordsman three times, but fell at the hands of the butcher. Then the crowd called the *espada* a buzzard, and other opprobrious names, and hurled oranges at him instead of cigars, as at the successful ones. This bull was finally lassoed and killed, and the eighth and last was let in. He had his horns padded, so that he could not gore anybody, and a crowd of beggars were let loose, who tormented him to their hearts' content. When the "sport" ended, the sun had dropped behind the western hills, and everybody was weary. We were disgusted and ashamed, but had sat through it all, and our Historian had even taken with his camera a series of instantaneous pictures of the fight.

"Well, boys," said the Judge, "we have now seen the famous national pastime of the Spaniards, that has amused them these hundreds of years. What do you think of it?"

And the reply was unanimous, that it was brutal, degrading, and revolting, and ought to be suppressed.

CHAPTER X.

CADIZ, GIBRALTAR, AND MALAGA.

SEVILLE, the Queen of Andalusia, is situated upon the river Guadalquivir, which flows majestically down to the Atlantic, coming to the ocean north of Cadiz, the next city we visited. The voyage down the river was interesting, but we anxiously looked for Cadiz; and at last out gleamed the city, white as a snow-drift, beautiful as a dream. We were not disappointed on landing, even though pounced upon and unmercifully robbed by the boatmen and porters; for in the first place we had our minds filled with the vision of loveliness that greeted us as we entered the harbor, and were in a state of serenity that defied the assaults of those mercenary Spaniards; and again, we had counted upon having no end of trouble in passing the customs, and reckoned anything short of robbery of all our goods as something to be expected. But the customs officials, who had it in their power to make it very uncomfortable for us, were excessively attentive and polite. They merely glanced at the top trays of our trunks, peeped into our largest valises, and ordered them on. Then that precious luggage was seized by seven stalwart beggars, who wrenched and twisted it in seven different ways at once, and then took it to the railroad station. Three of them carried the baggage, and four more went along to see them do it, and to claim payment for that superintendence. So glad were we to enter Cadiz at so little cost, that we paid them their price, much

CADIZ.

to their astonishment, and evidently to their dissatisfaction. Then, bribing a railroad porter to keep watch over said luggage until we should be ready to depart, we entered the city and sought a hotel.

Cadiz is charming and clean. So clean were the streets, so white the houses, so beautiful the glimpses of guarded courts and *patios*, so freshly green the blinds and *jalousies*, that we fell in love with it over again. We don't think we shall ever forget — at least we hope not — our walk along the *alameda*, fronting the open sea, nor the glorious sunset-clouds, nor the ramble along the battlements in the freshness of the following morning. Cadiz is a walled city, with sea-walls and vast fortifications, and one may walk more than a mile along the inner battlements, with views of the sea on one hand, and on the other fine old houses and narrow streets, — peeping through loop-holes and narrow slits in ornate sentry-boxes upon such bits of marine life as would keep an artist employed an entire season in depicting. And then the air of antiquity over the gray walls, despite the fresh appearance of the city proper, despite the cleanliness!

The situation of Cadiz, commanding the entrance to a magnificent bay whose farther shores are rather dim, upon a neck of land close fortified and separated from the back country by a river and marshes, with unobstructed ocean navigation even to the eastern shores of the New World, early called attention to this Phœnician city as the great seaport of western and southern Spain. When, after the first voyage of Columbus had opened the way to America, great preparations were made for his second voyage, Cadiz was selected as the port of embarkation, though the ships were fitted out in Seville. A glorious spectacle must those seventeen ships have presented as they assembled in the harbor with their freightage of rich stuff, and receiving aboard the best of Spain's offerings in the way of proud *hidalgos*, soldiers, and *caballeros*, fresh from fighting the Moors, Andalusian steeds, armor, and armament. The ships of Columbus sailed proudly out, but the commander never so proudly sailed again; only seven years later, in 1500, Columbus returned to this same port in chains. This, however, was at the end of his third voyage, in December, 1500. From the recently-won city of Granada, Ferdinand and Isabella sent commands that the chains should be removed, and that the dishonored admiral should appear in their presence. To Cadiz also came the spoils of the second voyage, — the gold and the captives, parrots, plants, and fruits, and the first Carib cannibals the Spaniards had taken. No coast city more important at that period than Cadiz; but it has fallen from its high place in the past four hundred years, and now struggles to support a population greater than its needs demand. This accounts for the fierce fights of the boatmen and porters over a stranger's luggage, and for the desperate competition for his patronage; the poor beggars have to fight for a living or capitulate to starvation.

Cadiz should certainly receive fame as a seaside resort for the winter and early spring, with its broad *paseos* and *alamedas*, its unsurpassed sea-views, its clean though narrow streets, its ancient architecture. The people here seem to appreciate its sea-views and *paseos;* for on the roof (or *azotea*) of nearly every house is perched a little tower or belvedere; and these little turrets break the outline of the city as seen from the sea, and give a character to its architecture. Climb the winding stairway of the Torre Vijia to its roof-top, and then feast your eyes upon the views presented on every hand, — white seas of stone-walled houses, divided by narrow streets, with a thousand turrets dotting the surface.

We cannot mention half the attractions of Cadiz (let the curious readers seek a guide-book), but the visitor should by all means ascend to the Torre Vijia and look about him. We now recall how gloriously the sun went down that afternoon into the western sea, darting his Parthian arrows at the marble city from behind the barrier of a thunder-cloud with sombre buttresses and golden battlements.

THE DEFEAT OF THE ARMADA.

As Sol (for that is his name here) sent his last sheaf of golden arrows at the tower, we pointed our camera at him and *shot him on the spot.* It is a great solace, that camera, as well as a great trouble. We have secured some fascinating pictures with it, and have made some most marvellous misses. The picture of Sol (if there be a picture) now rests in obscurity; but we hope soon, with the application of proper chemicals, to bring his countenance to the light of his own beams. Speaking of pictures, there are many oil-paintings here in Cadiz, and enough Murillos to make the fortune of a small gallery in the United States, could it but possess them. The Museum has two or three of them, but the best are in the chapel of the ancient convent of Santa Catalina.

The finest one there is perhaps the San Antonio; but the one to which most interest is attached is the large painting behind the altar, which the artist was at work upon when he received a fall which eventually caused his death. While painting this picture he fell from the scaffolding and was so injured that he repaired at once to Seville, the place of his birth and scene of his greatest labors, where he died in 1682, at the age of sixty-four. This painting, then, was probably his last work. Left unfinished, it was completed by a pupil. From the wealthy merchants and monasteries of Cadiz, Murillo received orders for some of his best pictures; but it is in Seville that we must look for the largest collection of his works in Andalusia. The Academy of Fine Arts in Cadiz issues an excellent catalogue, which makes up for the deficiencies of works of art by detailed description. The Academy contains a great many paintings well worth the student's attention.

Wishing to photograph this last work of Murillo, we received permission from the *capellan* of the convent to do so, although it was on a feast-day, and the little chapel was well filled with worshippers. We will confess to some misgivings as to the correctness of our proceedings, — photographing a picture in the *retable mayor* before which silent figures draped in black were kneeling in adoration. But they paid less attention to us than we to them, and took it as a matter of course, sanctioned as it was by the *capellan*, who accompanied us and the sacristan, who opened wide the great, creaking doors that more light might enter.

We had heard much of the fanaticism and jealous scrutiny of strangers to be encountered in Spain; but after three months in the land we can say we have yet to meet them. All have received us as did the gentle and courteous chaplain of the convent; and whatever the *religiosos* may have been in times past, they are now to all outward appearances tolerant and even liberal.

Leaving Cadiz one morning, we set out, on a roundabout journey, for Malaga, by the way of Tangiers in Morocco, and Gibraltar. A little steamer makes the voyage twice a week between Cadiz and Tangiers in about ten hours. We are not going to describe Tangiers, nor any part of Africa which we afterward visited (though we explored Algiers as well, and went down into the interior, toward the great desert of Sahara), for that story belongs to our adventures in North Africa. One famous point we passed, midway between Cadiz and Tangiers, where all our English passengers took off their hats and allowed their usually impassive countenances to glow with exultation. For this point was Trafalgar, where, in 1805, Lord Nelson gained the victory and lost his life, after twice crossing the ocean to meet the combined French and Spanish fleets. Finally, the point of Tarifa, with its white tower blazing against great drifts of yellow sand, again flamed out to us a welcome to Spain. But the channel was very rough, the cross winds from the Atlantic and the Mediterranean rolling up a very disagreeable sea. About three hours of this rough sailing brought us into smoother waters, and we could then enjoy the coast views rapidly unrolled as we steamed along.

To that land of mysteries, whence came the wild invaders of Spain a thousand years ago, — to sun-scorched Africa, our steamer's

prow was turned, and in a few hours we anchored in the open road-
stead of Tangiers. Now, it is far from our purpose to describe
Tangiers, or our stay there, for reasons already given. Suffice it;
Tangiers completed our pictures of the Arabs domiciled in the north

TRAFALGAR BAY.

of Africa, and with our mental vision dwelling upon scenes Oriental
and architecture of the time of the Moorish invasion, we turned our
steps toward the desired land of the Spaniards again. Six hours'
steaming brought us over to Gibraltar. Glorious rock of Gibraltar,
— most magnificent of any part of the coast scenery of either Spain

or northern Africa! The great rock rose before us, as we glided
into its cool shadows, with long serrated crest, green and gray, with
pink and yellow houses nestling at its base, with heavy cloud-masses
hanging over Spain beyond, and with a glimpse of the silver Sierra
Nevadas.

We had two hours on shore, and those two hours were well
improved, ransacking the town for views and *curios*, and peering into
all out-of-the-way corners. No, we did n't have time to climb the
rock, nor did we see any monkeys, save such as we had brought
with us of the species that walked erect on two legs, and rejoiced in
the name of man. Before we sailed away from Gibraltar we could
not fail to note its grand and beautiful harbor, where all the ships
of the world might come to anchor, between the rock and the
opposite low-lying coast of Spain.

The pleasantly-situated Spanish towns San Roque and Algeciras
threw out their white walls,—one against a broad green plain, and the
other against the sky. Cool and comfortable lay the town at the base
of the rock, until about nine o'clock; then the sun had climbed above
its crest, and changed the climate of the pleasant town from temperate
to torrid. Above the white houses of the modern town of "Gib"
rises the ruined tower of the Moors, and this gray fortress carries us
back to a period more remote than that of the acquisition of Gibraltar
by the English; for these only came into possession in 1704, and the
town dates from away back in the dark ages. When the Goths had
possession of Spain, they also held in Africa the important posts of
Ceuta, Tangiers, and Arsilla. Ceuta, the Spaniards hold to-day. These
garrisoned places held back the Mohammedan sea of migration for
more than a century; but finally, through the defection of a Gothic
chieftain, the first waves of the Arab conquest lapped against the
Rock of Gibraltar. A reconnoitring force under Tarif (from whom
was named the town of Tarifa, which we can see from Gibraltar
shining on the other shore) felt its way cautiously along the coast

THE ROCK OF GIBRALTAR.

of Spain,— five hundred Africans and Arabs. They came back to Africa and reported to their commander, and then was sent over Tarah, who gave the name to Gibraltar — Gibel-al-tarik — the Rock of Tarah. He landed with five thousand soldiers, and, making Gibraltar his base of operations, effected finally the conquest of the greater portion of Spain.

Farther back still in the history of the world's peoples "old Gib" takes the speculative student of history, even to that remote time when the Atlantic was unknown to the dwellers along the Mediterranean shores, and this great rock formed, with the opposing promontory of Ceuta, the far-famed Pillars of Hercules. Have not these pillars been stamped upon the coins of Spain since times remote, and are they not stamped there to-day? You may still find them, one on either side the arms and royal crown of Spain, but the motto encircling them is not the same as it was in olden times. Columbus changed it for the Spaniards; until some four hundred years ago it was *Ne plus ultra.* The ancients regarded the Pillars of Hercules as the farthest bounds of their world, at least, of Spain. It was Charles V., we think, who adopted the modern motto, *Plus ultra,* in place of the antiquated one.

Americans may take an interest in these Pillars of Hercules from the fact that they constitute the standards of our dollar-mark, thus : S. If we go back far enough, step by step, we shall come to the time when Atlantis was believed in, and when the Greeks gave credence to the story related to Solon by the wise Egyptian priests of the existence in mid-ocean of a terrestrial paradise.

Eight hours more of steaming took us to Malaga. Another night of sailing over waters tolerably smooth, and we awoke in sight of land. Before us, in the cool shadows of hills, beyond which the sun had not yet risen, lay Malaga, city of raisins and wines. The hills were dimpled and uneven, mainly bare of trees, apparently not much cultivated, yet numerously dotted with the white walls of farm

and country houses. And thus we came around to Spain again after
preliminary voyaging, having flanked it on its western side, and
marched upon it from the land of its ancient enemies the Moors.

Though we had come thus unexpectedly upon the country, the inhabitants, such of them (and there were many) as came to meet us,
were not at all confounded. As soon as our anchor had dropped,
a gunshot from the lighthouse on the mole, the sea was swarm-
ing with boats of every description, containing ravenous boatmen
anxious to carry us to the shore. Their hungry looks, their violent
demonstrations, augured ill for the character of the people they
represented. All looked half-starved, poverty-stricken, driven by
wretchedness to the verge of desperation. Nor did their looks belie
their character; for a more wretched lot of vagabonds than those who
swarm the streets of Malaga would be difficult to find.

There are few things here deserving the attention of a stranger;
certainly there is nothing in Malaga worth a special journey to see.
And it is one of the dirtiest cities we saw. The streets of the city
are in bad condition, the *plazas* are neglected, and the roads leading into the country are horrible to experience. There is a grand
cathedral here, containing beautiful windows, and organs famous for
their carvings. Malaga's interest centres in its past, and pertains
to the people from whom the city was wrested four hundred years
ago. To us, indeed, the Spain of the past, of the long ago, is far
more interesting than that of to-day; for we see now merely the
decaying remnants of a once powerful nation dwelling in the habita-
tions from which their ancestors drove a people in many respects
superior to themselves. Spain, like that odd crustacean the hermit-
crab, dwells in the abandoned shell of another.

But as to the history of Malaga; at one point, at least, it impinges
upon that of the Christian world. Time was when Malaga was a
flourishing place, the principal seaport of the province Granada, the
sea in front active with the commerce of the Moors, and the hills and

slopes behind covered with vineyards and gardens. Long before this period it was a port of call of the Phœnicians, and is said to have its name from *Malak* (place of salt). Its beautiful bay, large and

SKETCH IN GIBRALTAR.

accessible, the tributary river, and the plains beyond the hills could not but have attracted the sails of voyagers from earliest times.

At the conquest of Spain by the Moors it became a city of importance, like Cartagena and Almeria; for right across the sea, not

far distant, lay Africa, the home of the Arab conquerors. To the
cities, towns, and fortified places of the mountains beyond it, which
send their spurs right down to the coast, Malaga was necessary, as
offering communication with Africa, through which came supplies and
troops. This was what hastened the downfall of Malaga; for the
King of Spain, Ferdinand, in his operations preliminary to his first
sieges of Granada and the Alhambra, deemed it necessary to cut off
all communication with Africa by capturing the ports of the Mediterranean. And so in 1487 Ferdinand the Catholic assembled his
forces for the investment of Malaga. With a large and well-appointed
army he penetrated the rugged Sierras that guard the seaports on the
landward side, the gloomy Alpuxarras.

Ferdinand did not directly assault the city of Malaga itself, but
first attacked and captured Velez Malaga, a town some two or three
leagues down the coast, whose white dwellings we could see as we
entered the bay. He was combated vainly by the old Moorish king,
El Zagal, who came thundering through the mountains from Granada
with a chosen troop. The Spaniards took the town and its crag-built
fortress, giving the wretched inhabitants leave to make shift as they
pleased, but taking away their homes. Then, when the flower of
Andalusian soldiery had gathered about his banner, when the coast
was white with the sails of assembling sailors anxious to share in the
spoils of a great city, Ferdinand marched upon Malaga. He closely
invested the city, by land and sea. But it was rich and well-stored,
with all the necessities and luxuries of life. Its walls were of great
strength, washed by the sea on one side, by a river on another, and
climbing the hills behind the town. The river-gate was defended
by two towers of strength; at the opposite and upper end of the
town, as it ran up the slopes of the eastern hill, was the vast citadel,
capable of holding thousands, known as the Alkazaba. Immediately
above the citadel was the impregnable fortress of Gibralfaro, anciently
a lighthouse, as its name indicates, — *Gibel-faro* (hill of the light-tower).

MALAGA.

This was connected with the Alkazaba by a zigzag staircase, covered and protected by thick walls; but as it crowned the apex of a steep hill it dominated both citadel and city.

The *alcaydes* of the city and citadel were empowered by the citizens to make an honorable capitulation, and had they succeeded, doubtless the fate of Malaga would have been less terrible. But the dominating fortress of the Gibralfaro was held by a fierce African Moor of the implacable tribe of Zegri, who never gave or expected quarter, and hated the Christians with a hatred only to be quenched in blood. Hamet el Zegri, as he was called, commanded a band of wild African warriors, equally fierce as himself. Their chieftain had not long since lost his mountain stronghold of Ronda to the Spaniards, and he was now determined to defend Malaga to the last. While the *alcayde* of the city was trying to make terms with Ferdinand, El Zegri descended to the Alkazaba, put its commander to death, and threatened the lives of all who should even whisper of capitulation to the Spaniards.

Then began the siege, and one of the most heroic defences mentioned in history. Heavy ordnance, mounted on the surrounding hills, and the batteries of the ships in the harbor, played incessantly upon the walls of citadel and fortress night and day, but without avail. Whenever a breach was made, the Moors erected another wall behind it, and repelled every assault with great carnage.

El Zegri and his Africans fought like demons; they made desperate sallies through the breaches opened by the enemy's cannon, and only relinquished their efforts when stark famine had worn them into weak submission. Not only El Zegri, but a famous Moorish *Santon* (or holy man), led them to savage slaughter, but in vain. At last El Zegri had recourse to the arts of the astrologer, and for days remained shut up in his loftiest tower, in consultation with a famous necromancer, who promised, when the right time should come, to lead the warriors forth to victory. The day did come; but the fierce onslaught was repelled, the sacred banner captured, the necromancer slain, and the best portion of El Zegri's soldiers bit the dust.

Famine completed what cannon and the sword began, and finally the city capitulated without terms, save that the inhabitants, such as could, should be allowed to ransom themselves from impending slavery. It came about, however, through the craftiness of Ferdinand, that hardly a score of the inhabitants escaped being sold as slaves. They were induced to give up all their gold and jewels in part payment for their ransom, with the promise that they should have freedom when the balance was made up by their friends. But it was never done. Ferdinand kept their treasures, and treacherously sold them all as slaves. A hundred of the best fighters were sent as a present to the Pope, Innocent VIII., and a hundred Moorish maidens were divided between the royal families of Spain and Portugal. Fifteen thousand Moors, men, women, and children, were thus sold into slavery by the "most Christian" king and the "gentle Isabella." The brave Hamet el Zegri died in a dungeon ; and thus the Spanish king got control of the southern coast of Spain.

To-day we may yet see the gray old Gibralfaro, still occupied by the soldiers of Spain ; but it looks out upon a city far from prosperous, — upon hillsides once crowned with hanging gardens, now but scantily cultivated. We found the old citadel, the Alkazaba, occupied by hundreds of families, numerous as crows, and nearly all as famished. In its ruins they had walled off for themselves little dens and rookeries, and here dwelt, looking out upon magnificent prospects over sea and land, but with filth and squalor all around. We climbed the steep hill beyond the citadel to the very gate of the grim castle ; but the only soldier on guard wouldn't let us in, and we had to content ourselves with rambling around the walls. They rise steep on every side, surrounded by deep ditches where the steepness of the hill did not preclude their necessity. A little way to the eastward is another mount, captured and held by the Marquis of

Cadiz, Rodrigo Ponce de Leon, around which the stormy battle fiercely raged.

Above the battlements rises a tower, which must be the same in which El Zegri held his mysterious consultation with the astrologer;

A SKETCH IN MALAGA.

and the covered way connecting castle and citadel (though no longer covered) may still be traced up the winding crest of the hill. The only other relic of the Moor that is prominent is a great arch erected at the entrance to the market-place. Our only chance companion on the hill, as we surveyed the fort, was a boy, who lay flat upon the ground all the while. Upon coming up to him we found that he was engaged in trapping birds; he had half a dozen cages arranged around a bare spot on the hillside, and strings leading from them and the snare he had spread, so that by pulling them he could cause the birds inside to flutter, and when strange birds had settled on his trap, he could also pull other strings and net them. Leaving our young bird-catcher to his pastime, we meandered back to the city and engaged seats in the train for Granada.

CHAPTER XI.

T Malaga we took a "new departure," inasmuch as we resolved to see more of the people and of social life than we had hitherto seen.

"We have now been together several weeks," said the Judge, "and so far as any intimate acquaintance with you goes, I am still a stranger to you and you are strangers to me. Now," continued he, beaming upon us with a friendly smile, "we must proceed to get better acquainted."

Both Professor and Historian assented heartily to this proposition. The fact is, we had been so very busy filling our time with sight-seeing, that we had (as the Judge said) passed very little time together. In our anxiety also to see the historic cities and cathedrals, palaces and monuments, the Spaniards themselves, the dwellers among these attractions, had been almost entirely neglected. As we took train for Granada, and had left behind us the ancient but muddy Malaga, we settled ourselves down to compare notes of our various journeys.

"I must confess," said our Historian, "that I did want to make one journey which we have omitted, and that was to Palos, whence Columbus first set sail for America, in 1492."

"Yes," assented the Judge, "that is a natural desire for an American, especially as the year (1892) draws nigh in which we are to celebrate the four hundredth anniversary of the alleged discovery of our land. Perhaps we may yet accomplish it, and go over ground I myself have visited."

"You! You have been there?" chimed in chorus the Professor and Historian.

STREET MUSICIANS.

"Yes indeed, and not many years ago."

"And is it still there, — the port, the Church of St. George, in which Columbus read the proclamation to the people, and the old convent? Tell us about it, please."

"Well, I will; though the scenery ahead of us is of the finest in Spain, and you must n't allow my story to divert your attention from these glorious mountains."

The Alpuxarras, the snow-covered peaks of Andalusia, were right before us, and the sun shining brightly upon their burnished shields. We promised, and the Judge proceeded: —

"At Seville, as you know, we saw many memorials of Columbus, and of those early voyages by famous Spaniards. After the second voyage of Columbus,

COLUMBUS.

in 1493, that city was the great fitting-out station for the fleets. From Seville, one day in April, I took train for a little station on the railroad called Huelva; but I was told by a fellow-passenger that I must go by the way of Moguer if I would visit the very route of Columbus as he himself went to Palos. So I sought it out, — a little sleepy town with a great church and an old convent. This convent, by the way, or the chapel attached to it, was the one to which Columbus and his sailors went to say their prayers after their return from America, in the fulfilment of a vow they had made at sea during a terrible storm. Here I saw, too, the ancestral dwelling of the Pinzons, those gallant captains who went with Columbus, and but for whom, doubtless, he would never have been able to get ships and sailors for his great expedition. Their descendants still reside there, though much to my regret I learned that the family was away; for I very much desired to grasp the hand of a Pinzon. No direct descendant of Columbus is now alive; but in my opinion the Pinzons were of better stock than the Great Admiral himself. My host at the little hotel furnished me with a boy and a donkey early next morning, and I set off for Palos, over an excellent road, all the way through carefully cultivated vineyards, and soon arrived there. The little village is a very wretched one, and is nearly half a mile from the Rio Tinto, the river in which Columbus gathered together his caravels for his voyage. But the Church of St. George is there yet, in good preservation; and I saw the veritable pulpit from which was read the royal proclamation commanding the people of Palos to furnish men and caravels for the mysterious voyage; likewise the great wooden image of Saint George and the dragon, which was there in the time of Columbus, if we may believe the local traditions.

"But nobody knew anything about either Columbus or his times, not even the *cura* (or parish priest), and so I pushed on three miles farther, to the convent. This is known as La Rabida, and stands on a high hill overlooking the Rio Tinto, and with a distant view of the sea. I approached the gateway and was welcomed by the *conserge* (or man in charge) at the very portal where Columbus had called for a drink of water for his child nearly four hundred years ago.

PEASANT.

"The building is still in good preservation, and probably as Columbus saw it, with many empty cloisters, where the monks then resided, a fine garden-patio in its centre, and a *mirador* (or balcony) with fine views of the coast. The old *conserge* was so pleasant and hospitable that I asked permission to stay overnight; and this being granted, I sent back my donkey and donkeyboy, and took possession. My friends were very poor, but kind and cheerful. I furnished the money, and they sent to Palos for some goat-meat and eggs. They gave me their best bed in one of the cloisters, and I passed altogether one of the pleasantest periods of my life.

"The chapel is still shown here of the good old prior of the convent, Padre Marchena, and the very room in which was held the famous consultation between him and Columbus and the learned doctor, which resulted in the prior's setting off on his mule to lay the case before Isabella. The result all the world knows now, — that Isabella was persuaded to promise assistance to Columbus, who went to her court, then held at Santa Fé, in the *vega* of Granada, and that the final result was the discovery of America. So you see these four places — Seville, Palos, La Rabida, and Granada, for which we are now destined — are joined in their connection with the history of America."

When the Judge had ceased speaking, a bright-eyed Spaniard who had occupied the opposite seat of our compartment addressed him in very good English, and asked if he had visited the great copper-mines of Huelva, on the opposite shore of the bay below Palos. The

QUEEN ISABELLA.

Judge said he had; and the Spaniard continued: "Those mines are said to have been worked by the Phœnicians two thousand years ago, and that coast is supposed to be the ancient Tarshish of the Bible. But, *señores,* though there is copper in these mountains all about us, there is that which is more precious still, — silver, and also gold. Yes, indeed, *hay plata y oro en abundancia* (gold and silver in abundance)"

Being encouraged by us, our new friend went on to relate stories of these hills that we eagerly made a note of as he rolled them out in the English he had acquired in America. " But, *señores*, most of my

COLUMBUS PUT IN IRONS.

life has been passed in Mexico, where I have been mining for many years. *There* you will find gold and silver, — if you but know where to look for it, — and quicksilver, and emeralds, rubies sometimes, and opals. Did your worships ever hear of the *veta negra*, the great black vein of silver that was worked for so many years, and then so suddenly disappeared? No? Then perhaps you would like me to tell it to you, — the story of its disappearance, as I learned it from an old *gambusino* (a poor miner) many years ago. Perhaps it may have been told in books before this; but I think not, as I myself do not recollect having told it to any English or Americans. This is it, if you will condescend to listen, — this is the story of this wonderful vein and its mysterious ending some fifty years ago : —

THE MINE-KING: A STORY OF MEXICO.

Ojala por los dias de oro ! — oh for the days of gold ! sighed the old *gambusino ; pero ya se acabó todo eso,* — but *that* is all over now ; *ni oro, ni plata hay,* — neither gold nor silver is to be had nowadays for picking or digging. *Pedazitos, no mas* — little bits one grubs up here and there ; *pero se acabó la veta negra,* — but the black vein, the black vein ; *onde está ?* — where is it ? Worked out, long ago.

I was no older than your worship, in those days, and my back was strong : *Válgame madre santíssima !* but I could pack the ore nimbly in the mine and up the shaft. Ay, and *then* all worked with a will, for it was all *bonanza ;* day after day, month after month, year after year, there we were, at the same old vein ; and the more we cut into it, the richer it grew. *Ay que plata !* Oh, what silver came out of that old vein ! *blanco, rico, pesado,* — white, rich, and heavy, it was, — all silver, all silver. Five hundred *pesos fuertes* I made in one week. *Que hermosita aquella veta negra !* — what a beautiful little vein was that black one !

But your worship yawns, and my poor old head turns round when it thinks of that time. *Pues señor.* All the miners (for there 'were no *gambusinos* then) were making dollars as fast as they could ; but the more they got the more they wanted, although not one of the laziest but had more than he ever before had dreamed of possessing. However, they were not satisfied, and all complained because they did not strike a richer vein than the old *veta negra,* — as if that were possible !

The most dissatisfied of all the miners was a little deformed man called Pepito, who did nothing but swear at and curse his bad luck, although he had made enough money to last three of his lives ; and the miserly style in which he lived was the by-word of everybody. However, whether it was from a bitterness of spirit caused by his deformity, or from genuine badness of heart, Pepito was continually grumbling at the old vein, calling it by every opprobrious epithet which he could summon to the end of his tongue, and which was enough to break the heart of any vein, even of iron.

One night — it was the *fiesta* of San Lorenzo — all the miners were away in the town, for they had agreed to give themselves a holiday; but Pepito took his basket and pick, and declared his intention of remaining to work; "for," said he, "what time have I for holiday, when with all my work, work, work, I only get enough out of that stony old vein to keep me in *frijolitos*, without a taste of *pulque* since — *quién sabe?* — how long ago ? *Maldita sea la veta, digo yo*, — curse such a vein, say I! *Válgame Dios !* — this to the black vein, the black vein of Sombrerete!" apostrophized the old *gambusino*.

Now your worship knows, of course (but *quién sabe?* for foreigners are great fools), that every mine has its metal king, its *mina padre*, to whom all the ore belongs. He is, your worship knows, not a man, nor a woman, but a spirit, and a very good one, if he is not crossed or annoyed; and when the miners curse or quarrel at their work, he often cuts off the vein, or changes it to heavy lead or iron; but when they work well and hard, and bring him a good stock of *cigarros*, or leave him in the gallery when they quit the mine a little bottle of *pulque* or *mescal*, then he often sends *bonanzas*, and plenty of rich ore.

Well, everybody said when they heard Pepito's determination to remain alone in the mine, and after he had so foully abused the celebrated *veta negra*, "*Válgame !* if Pepito does n't get a visit from *padre mina* to-night, it 's because he has borrowed holy water or a *rosarioncite* from Father José, the *cura* from Sombrerete."

We were all going to work again at midnight, but the *mezcal* was so good that none stirred from the *pulqueria* until long after that hour. I, however, shouldered my pick and trudged up the hill to the shaft, first waking up the watchman, who lay snoring at the gate of the *hacienda*, wrapped in his *serape*. I took him with me to the mouth of the shaft, that he might lower me down in the basket; and down I went. When I got to the bottom I called to Pepito, — for, knowing he was working there, I had not brought a lantern, — but heard nothing save the echo of my own voice sounding hollow and loud as it vibrated through the passages and galleries of the mine. Thinking he might be asleep, I groped my way to where we had been working the great lode in the morning, hoping to find him in that direction, and hallooing as I crept, but still no answer; and when I shouted, "Pepito, Pepito, *onde está ?* — where are you?" the echo cried jeeringly, "*Onde está ?*"

At length I began to get frightened. Mines, everybody knows, are full of devils and gnomes, and bad spirits of every kind; and here was I, at midnight, alone, and touching the "black vein" which had been so abused. I did not like to call again to Pepito, for the echo frightened me, and I felt assured that the answer was made by some unearthly voice, and came direct from the lode of the *veta negra* that we were working. I crept back to the bottom of the shaft, and looking up to the top, where the sky showed no bigger than a *tortilla*, with one bright star looking straight down, I shouted to the watchman to lower

the basket and draw me up; but, holy mother! my voice seemed to knock itself to pieces on the sides of the shaft as it struggled up, and when it reached the top must have been a whisper. I sat down and fairly cried, when a loud shout of laughter rattled along the galleries, and broke as it were up the shaft; I trembled like quicksilver, and heavy beads of perspiration dropped from my forehead to the ground. There was another shout of laughter, and a voice cried out, "Come here, Matthias; come here."

"Where, most wonderful señor?" I asked, thinking it well to be respectful.

"Here, here to the black vein, — the old leaden, useless vein," cried the voice, mockingly; and I thought with horror of the abuse it had that day received.

Half dead with fear, I crept along the gallery, and turning an abrupt angle, came upon the lode we had been working. *Ave María purissima!* what a sight

met my eyes! The gallery seemed a mass of fire, yet there was no blaze and no heat. The rock which contained the vein of ore, and the ore itself, were like solid fire ; and yet it was n't fire, for there was no heat, as I said, but a glare so bright that one could see away into the rock, which seemed to extend miles and miles, and every grain of quartz, and even the smallest particle of sand, of which it was composed, was blazing with light, and shone separately, like a million diamonds knocked in one ; and yet the eye saw miles into the bowels of the

ON MULEBACK.

earth, and every grain of sand was thus lighted up. But if the stone and the grit and the sand were thus fiery bright, and the eye was scorched to look upon it, what words can describe the glitter of the vein, now of sparkling silver, and white as it were with flame, but over which a black blush now and then shot, and instantaneously disappeared? It wanted not this, however, to tell me that I was looking at the endless *veta negra*, the scorned, abused black vein, which throbbed, miles and miles away into the earth, with virgin silver enough to supply the world for worlds to come.

"Ha, ha, ha!" roared the voice; "the old leaden, useless vein! Where is the man that can eat all this silver's worth of *frijolitos ?* Bring him here ! bring him here!" And forthwith a thousand little sparkling figures jumped out of the scintillating rock, and springing to the ground, ringing like new-coined *pesos*, they seized upon the body of Pepito, which I had not till now observed, who lay, blue with fear, in a corner of the gallery, and lifting him on their shoulders, brought him in front of the silver vein. The brightness of the metal scorched his eyes, which still could not, even in his fear, resist feasting on the richness of the glittering lode.

"*Bonanza, una bonanza !*" shouted the enraptured miner, forgetting his situation and the presence he was in; for the figure (if figure it can be called which was like a mist of silver fire) of the *padre mina* (the mine-king) was now seen sitting in state on the top of the vein.

"*Bonanza!*" shouted the same voice derisively; "*bonanza* from an old leaden, useless vein!" repeating the terms which Pepito had used in abusing it. "Where's the man can eat this silver's worth of *frijolitos?* What does he deserve who has thus slighted the silver king? Turn him to lead, lead, lead!" answered the voice. "Away with him, then."

The thousand sparkling silverines seized the struggling miner. "Not lead, not lead," he shouted; "anything but lead!" But they held him fast by the legs, and bore him opposite the lode. The rock sparkled up into a thousand times more brilliant coruscation than before, and for an instant I thought my eyes would have burned with looking at the silver vein, so heavenly bright it shone. An instant after a void remained in the rock, — a horrid black void. The vein had disappeared, but the rock itself was still as bright as ever, — all but the black opening which yawned from out the brightness; and opposite this stood the thousand silverines, bearing the body of the luckless *gambusino.*

"*Uno! dos! tres!*" shouted the mine-king; and at the word "*tres,*" with a hop, skip, and jump, right into the gaping hollow spring the thousand silver-ines, with the luckless miner on their shoulders, whose body, the instant that his heels disappeared into the opening, with these very eyes I saw turned to lead.

Santa Maria! then all became dark, and I fell senseless to the ground. When I recovered a little, I thought to myself, Now will come my turn; but hoping to conciliate the angry mine-king, I sought in the breast of my shirt for a bottle of *mezcal,* which I remembered I had brought with me. There was the bottle, but without a single drop of liquor. This puzzled me; but when I called to mind the fiery spectacle I had just witnessed, I felt no doubt that the liquor had been dried up in the bottle by the great heat.

However, I was not molested, and in a short time the miners returned to the work, and finding me pale and trembling, called me *tonto, borracho,* — drunk and mad. We proceeded to the lode and grubbed away, but all we suc-ceeded in picking out were a few lumps of poor lead ore; and from that day not a dollar's worth of silver was ever drawn from the famous black vein of Sombrerete.

Our Spanish companion was so very agreeable, and had such a fund of amusing stories about the country, as well as a store of his-

toric information, that we were much pleased to learn that he was
going through with us to Granada. He handed us his card in
exchange for our own "pasteboards," and we read, "Tomas Merino y
Borrér," — " *a servicio de ustedes, caballeros*," he added, with a graceful
bow, — " at your service, gentlemen." Generally speaking, this is an
empty compliment; but we found that Don Tomas meant all he said.
Having been in America, he had a great liking for *Americanos*.
The Judge, especially, he doubly liked, since they could converse
together in Spanish, which was much more agreeable to him than
the English. He indicated to us the picturesque and historic features
of the country, as we passed, advising us to go to Ronda, the most
picturesque town in Spain. But Ronda was nearly two days' diligence from the railroad, and we had no time. There was one place
we should have liked to visit, and that was Zahara, which has a
history most fascinating. It was the unfortunate town captured by
the Moorish king four hundred years ago, which was the cause of
the Moors being expelled from Spain. So barbarous was the treat-
ment he gave the people of Zahara, that ever since that the Spaniards
have been greatly incensed. The brave Marquis of Cadiz, finding
that the truce was broken between the Moorish and the Spanish
kings, attacked and captured Alhama, and held it, despite the efforts
of the Moors to regain it; and this was the immediate cause of the
downfall of Granada itself. So our time was beguiled until the train
rolled into the station of Boabdilla, and we alighted for lunch, and to
change cars for the direct line to Granada.

CHAPTER XII.

E came out of the station at Boabdilla just in time to see our Spanish friend fall into the arms of another native of the land, and kiss him on both cheeks. Then after hugging him, and being hugged in return, he dragged him up to us and introduced him as a most illustrious descendant of a noble house, with whom he had lived and travelled in Mexico. His name was Angel Fadrique Gonzalez, with a Señor and Don prefixed, and as many titles affixed as you can string across this page. But he was a jolly, large-hearted gentleman, just the same, though he could n't speak English. He, too, was going to Granada ; so our party, now five in number, secured a compartment to itself, and we passed the time in telling stories and recalling the history of the places through which we passed.

The first town of importance we came to was Antequara, a city so ancient that it was founded on Roman ruins, and which lies near a great cave guarding prehistoric remains. It has a castle and a mosque, and near it is a great rock called *el Peñon de los Enamorados* (or the Lovers' Leap). According to a tradition, a Spanish captive escaped from the Moors, and with him a Moorish maiden who had fallen in love with him, were driven up this great rock by a party of pursuing Moors. Seeing no trace of mercy in the faces of the infuriate pursuers, they leaped to death, from the summit of the rock, clasped in each other's arms.

Our companions were fuller of Mexico than of Spain, and related many narratives of adventure there. Don Angel gave us one, in Spanish, which his friend translated for us, and the Historian transcribed. Perhaps the language of the noble Don may seem a little florid; but that may be the fault of the translator, or of our plain and every-day English. Here it follows; and Don Angel called it —

THE STORY OF A SHEPHERD-BOY.

LEAPING at once from his hiding-place beneath the waters of the Atlantic, the morning sun first bathed his face in a rosy cloud hanging on the horizon ready to receive him, then peered above its upper rim and darted at the world his brightest beams. The first of land objects struck by his fiery darts was Orizaba, the snow-mountain, whose silver helmet was soon suffused with crimson, that spread down upon his shoulders with fainter glow, touching the lava fields and flooding his forest-covered breast with molten gold. Higher and higher rose the sun, and deeper and deeper sank his golden shafts into the dim recesses of the forest.

The silent wilderness, feeling its gloom dispelled, bestirred itself to greet the coming of the day. In the topmost boughs of the trees its song-birds sat; thence they sent forth their joyful notes, warning the dwellers below — the parrots, monkeys, troupials — that their dusky sanctums were soon to be invaded. They, too, swelled the chorus with their cries, and ere long all Nature was awake. The last to receive the message of the morning was the great cañon of Palo Santo, which ran down the mountain-side towards the coast. Above its highest walls the forest trees crowded together and peered over them into the profound abyss but as it broadened out and the walls fell down lower and lower, the trees fled away, fearful perhaps of being engulfed and carried off by the stream that roared round the rocks in the chasm. The sun's rays fell slantwise across the cañon, illuming its western wall, but leaving the eastern in deepest shadow. The agaves on the western brink were changed to glistening candelabra, with their branching spikes of blossoms; the gray cacti showed all their fluted columns, the prickly pears their crimson flowers. Steadily crept the shadow of the eastern down the western wall, as the sunbeams searched for the foaming waters of the stream within the chasm. The trumpet-

BALCONIES OF GRANADA.

trees, with great leaves of green and silver, were quickened into life again, and tremulously shook off their burden of pearly dewdrops upon the orchids and the dank earth underneath.

Just where the crowns of the trumpet-trees reached the summit platform of one of the lower cliffs a broad ledge jutted from it, overarched by impending rock. Here, sheltered from observation by protecting rock and trees, reposed a little hut of clay, built like a swallow's nest against the wall. Its only aperture, the doorway, opened eastward, and its occupants were early awake, to receive the first glow from the sky. They were two in number, — an old man and a boy, whose complexions of golden bronze showed the noble Indian blood of the ancient tribe of the Totonacas. The boy was the first to emerge, drawing about him a coarse woollen *sarapito* (or Mexican blanket), his only other garment being his white cotton pantaloons. His face was bright as the sun that shone against it, his great black eyes were wide open with frankness and innocence, his red lips parted in a smile that showed his white and beautiful teeth. He could not have exceeded ten years of age, yet he had in his bearing the self-poise of a man full grown.

"*Padre mio,*" he said, in low, sweet tones, "wilt thou not rise, father mine, and come out into the sunshine ? Come and sit in the sun, while I go down to the river."

"Yes, my little son; but come and lead your father into the light. *El sol* is bright, I doubt not, but I can only feel his heat, and never more see his brightness."

"True, little father; I would that thou hadst one of Bernalito's eyes, and he one the less; it troubles me to see thee sit in darkness."

The boy led his aged, sightless parent through the doorway, and to a rock in the sun.

"There, *padrecito,* rest awhile; I will soon return."

The blind man sank to his seat with a sigh, while his son leaped down a rock-hewn stairway to the river, nearly one hundred feet below. After bathing face and hands, he dipped out a calabash of water, and hastened with it up the steep. Then he quickly lighted a fire, and prepared some *atolli* (or corn gruel), which served as their simple breakfast. Having swept out their hut and set near his father food and drink for the day, he made ready to depart, swinging over his shoulder a sack of tiger-skin containing some parched corn and strips of dried beef.

"*Adios, padrecito ;* Bernalito must leave thee now, for the sheep are calling from the corral. Dost need anything more ?"

"No, my little son, my only jewel, thy father needs nothing more — save

that the good Master in heaven send him rest; for truly, life alone, and in darkness, is wearisome."

The tears sprang to Bernalito's eyes as he kissed his father's brow and
smoothed back the whitened hair. Taking his face in his hands a moment,
and imprinting another kiss, he picked up his sling and staff, and swiftly went
away.

"*Adios!*" he cried from the rock steps. "Look for my coming when the
sun leaves thee in shadow."

The old Indian remained motionless, his face set in an expression of hope-
less sorrow. Two years had passed since blindness had fallen upon him; his
days were spent in solitude, helpless, upon the cliff. His sole possession was
a little flock of sheep and a garden beyond the woods, the entire care of which
now fell upon Bernalito. He drove the flock into the meadows every morning,
and watched them all day long, with no other companion except his little dog.
Now and then he left his sheep to themselves, and worked manfully in the half-
wild forest garden. With his sling he sometimes secured birds and rabbits,
which supplied them with their only meat, except an infrequent strip of dried
beef (or *tassajo*).

But notwithstanding his lonely life of unremitting toil, Bernalito was
happy; his only sorrow was his father, and even for him he looked hopefully
into the future.

"If I could only reach the great *Médico* of Cordova," he thought, as he
descended the cliff, "and bring that learned doctor to see *padrecito*, his sight
might be restored. But it would cost much money, I fear, more than four
pesos, — all I have; but then, four dollars is a great sum; that ought to pay
the *Médico* for his medicine. If I can but add another *peso* to it, I will go
to see him."

Farther down the cañon, where the great walls were spread apart with a
broader space between, was the corral, — a pen with walls of rock and a wicket
gate. As Bernalito opened the gate, his little flock poured forth tumultuously,
and took the narrow path to the pasture-land, while Fidencio, the nightly
guardian of the fold, leaped upon him and frisked about with barks of welcome. The boy was glad to see his sheep again; he followed them to the
rocky pasture, and sat down, while Fidencio lay at his feet. The dog was
puzzled, for his master had not received him with his usual cheerful greeting;
he winked his big brown eyes sorrowfully, while his ears drooped and his tail
hung limp. Bernalito was revolving a scheme in his mind, — a scheme by
which his father might have news of the *Médico* that very week. He would
leave Fidencio to care for the sheep, and go to the garden and there dig out

A FAMILY OF MENDICANTS.

yams enough to sell in Cordova on the next day. At the same time he would contract with the doctor to cure his father's blindness. There seemed to him no wiser plan ever conceived in the world, and he hastened to put it into execution. Fidencio received his orders gravely enough, and sat up erect on a rock, where he could command a view of the pasture; but he followed with asking eyes the movements of his master, and entirely ignored the morsel of meat left for his dinner.

An hour later, Bernalito was in the garden beyond the forest, where he began to work without delay. It was more difficult labor than he had expected, for the wilder vegetation had almost taken possession of the garden, and nearly choked out the maize and banana plants by their rank luxuriance of growth. So the day drew near its ending, the backload of yams was gathered, and when these had been collected and carried (in a netted sack of twine) to the verge of the clearing, there was little daylight left. Darkness was already settling upon the path, and in the gorges below it was quite black when he had deposited his burden at the point selected. It was not far from the forest path to Cordova, and he thought he would run over to it for a

CHATTO DIAZ.

moment. As he drew near a bank above the intersection of the two trails, he heard the sound of a human voice, and halted, drawing into deeper shade; for voices seldom broke the silence of those woods at that hour. The road to Cordova, merely a footpath deep-worn by the tread of Indians for centuries, was below him some twenty feet. Thence the sounds proceeded; and by looking over carefully, concealed as he was by wild plantains and the general gloom, he saw the owners of the voices, — two men huddled together in a hollow of the bank. One of them was then lighting a cigarette, and as the flame of the match lit up his face, bringing out strongly every feature, Bernalito drew back swiftly into the shade, clutching at his breast, as though to still the loud throbbing of his heart.

"*Dios mio !*" he uttered under his breath; "that is none else than Chatto Diaz, the *guerillero* of the mountains !"

He crouched in his hiding-place like a frightened squirrel, his slender frame trembling violently.

This *guerillero* (or bandit), Chatto Diaz, was the terror of the region, — an outlaw whose crimes were greater than those of any other in the country. Like the puma, the mountain lion, he delighted in deeds of blood merely for the pleasure of committing them. All dreaded him, — all, rich and poor; the wealthy *hacendado* and the lowly *peon*, — for he killed merely for the sake of killing.

"What can I do?" tremblingly inquired Bernalito of himself. "If he sees me, he will kill me, as he did my poor Juanito, when he met him and dashed him into the cañon. But why is he here? Perhaps — hush ! they are speaking together again."

The two bandits smoked awhile in silence, then one addressed the other: "How does *el capitan* know that he will come this way to-night?"

"No matter how I know," responded the captain. His companion did not call him Chatto, the flat-nose, for that was a name only used beyond his hearing.

"What is that to you? But he is coming, and soon, with his saddle-bags full of gold from the mine in the *corro*, and his *mozo* behind him driving a cargo mule heavy laden with silver."

"But why kill him? Why not lasso him, tie him to a tree, and make for the lava-beds? He cannot take us !"

Chatto blew forth a whiff of smoke directly into his comrade's face. "That for thy fears !" he growled. "Know you not that dead men make less trouble than living?"

"*Es verdad* (it is true)," quickly assented the other: "but Señor Ancona never did me any ill; though if you will kill him I shall offer no objection."

"I will make short work of him, don't you fear; you may have the *mozo* as yours."

"But when shall we meet him, and where?"

"At the ford, where the great cliff ends the cañon. He takes the cross-trail, to shorten his journey; and faith, it will be shorter than he thinks !"

"At the ford !" gasped Bernalito, with white lips in horror apart; "where our little house looks down upon the river, — they will do murder there! O my *padrecito!* But when?"

"*Bueno capitano!* Very good; we will stop him there. Two hours from now, did you say?"

"*Si,* that I said. Leave the horses here; it is only an hour through the forest. Hist! I heard a noise above us! Is any one here?"

"Oh, no; nobody in these forests, except old Manuel, the blind man, who lives in the cañon somewhere near the ford."

"*Bien!* If he is very near we may have the pleasure of seeing him fly over his own cliff-tops. *Caramba!* I remember his hut, half-way up the farther cliff. Surely, we are in luck to-night. I have it now; we will drop *el señor* Ancona at the foot of his stairway, and that will be a rich time when the *alcalde* finds him there. It would be better to see the old rascal dragged off to jail than to spill his blood, — much as I would like to do that. I would n't miss that part of the play. I will hide in the rocks and see it performed."

The saturnine Chatto chuckled, and smacked his lips; but Bernalito, as he heard this dreadful revelation, lay prone upon the ground, his young life nearly crushed out of his body. Had his own life been the only one at stake, he might then and there have lost consciousness, for the night was black with horror; but his senses recovered when he felt that his father's life was menaced. Not for himself, for others he must act at once; he slowly withdrew from the bank. It was quite dark, but the trail was too familiar for him to lose it; though he could not be aware of the exact location of every palm-leaf in it, and, despite his caution, stepped on one that crackled loudly. The bandits had risen from their smoke-talk, and were then going toward their horses; but the noise, slight as it was, startled them. Chatto rushed up to the bank, but only in time to note a receding formless figure.

"*Hola!*" he shouted. "Halt! I fire!"

No sooner said, than the flash of his revolver was followed by a report, but the fleeing figure did not stop.

"Follow me, Pedro. Our game is up unless we stop this *perillo.* On now, quick!"

Bernalito had an advantage in his perfect knowledge of the trail, but scarcely less accurate was that of the bandit, who had prowled through these woods for years. He was heavier, though, and encumbered by boots and accoutrements, while the prey he pursued was lightly clad.

"*O padrecito mio!*" panted the boy. "If I can but save thee and then the señor! What must I do, — go to thee first or to the stranger? *Dios mio,* — Father in heaven, — help thou Bernalito!"

He could hear the terrible, heavy breathing of Chatto crashing through the fallen branches and stumbling over the stones; but steadily the noise of pursuit grew fainter. The cañon was reached: down among the water-worn bowlders he plunged, leaping from one to the other; then he was out again, at the foot of the cliff on which the dwelling rose: he could see the wall behind it, in the faint light of the rising moon. He listened. Down below in the corral the sheep were bleating. Did he not hear his father's voice feebly calling? His little heart felt about to burst; but he resolutely held back all inclination to climb the cliff, and decided to go on to warn the stranger. Swiftly was this conclusion reached, for beyond the stream he could hear again the noise made by his pursuer. He fled on, climbing

THE BANDIT PEDRO.

the trail leading into the thither forest above the cañon.

"O father mine," he sobbed, "what am I leaving you to? May the good God direct me to do what is right! What if *el señor* should not come? Then all will be merely lost. Then I go back to die!"

It was too late to do else than keep on. If he had climbed the cliff to lead out his father, Chatto would have been at the ford before he could have hidden. No, there was nothing else to do. But what if Señor Ancona should be late? What if he should be a coward and return?

These thoughts appalled him; but on he went, torn and bleeding from the thorny vines of the wood, his strength fast failing. Could he reach the coming traveller—and was he coming? Chatto, the flat-nose, floundered through the flood, and sank breathless at the base of the precipice. His companion reached the bank he had left ere he went on again.

"Ho, there, Pedro, is that you? Yes? Then come over here and seat yourself, while I go some farther on. If I don't catch that whelp that listened, we may as well go back. Who is he, think you?"

Pedro reached him and sat down by his side. "I don't know," he said, "but have a thought that it is Manuel's boy, though he is young. Did you see him?"

"No, not plainly. Would my pistol miss him, if I had seen him?"

"True, *capitan*. I beg your pardon. What now?"

Chatto scowled blackly, communing with his evil thoughts. "What now?" he said at last. "Why, *blood! perdido*. Whose? Well, it will be useless to follow the unknown. Ancona and his gold are lost to us to-night. *Whose* blood, then, do you say? Whose but the Indian's? Wait awhile, till I breathe more steadily; then we will climb these stairs, and toss the old *ciego* over the brink."

"But, *capitan*, he has not injured us; he has no gold. Why not press on after the *hacendado*?"

"*Perdito!* Not hurt us! Who else was it but his son that spoiled our plans? No gold, you say; I do not always kill for gold; something redder than gold pleases me most! As for Ancona, when he hears that I am here in waiting for him, he turns back; and the boy, he cannot stay long away; we will feed him to the cray-fish of the cañon! *Vamos!* up the rocks! Toss old Manuel over and I will catch him on my *machete*."

"Bernalito!"

"Hark! he *is* there; hear him, calling his boy, perhaps. Oh yes, Bernalito is coming. Stay here, Pedro; let me have the pleasure of this affair."

Swinging along at a swift walk, the horse of Señor Ancona was bearing his rider rapidly toward the cañon. A few rods more, and he would emerge from the wood and pick his way down the trail among the rocks. It was lighter there, for the moon was well up in the sky, and Señor Ancona looked forward to that bit of moonlight gratefully, for the forest was very dark and grewsome. Suddenly his horse stops and snorts in alarm. The rider, hastily gripping the bridle-rein, looking up, sees a dusky form standing before him, with head raised. His own hand quickly grips the pistol in its holster, and he cries out, *Hola!* What do you want?"

"It is I, Bernalito," replies the one addressed, in a strained, quivering voice; and then he runs forward and lays a hand on the stirrup nearest him.

"They are below in the cañon, — Chatto and a *compañero;* they seek to kill you, *señor.*"

"Me! Chatto there! He would kill me if he should meet me in such a place. Get up, then, behind me, and we will ride back. Quick! give me your hand."

"Oh, no, *señor,*" fearfully cried the boy; "no, don't go back; my father is there, and they will kill him."

"Who is your father, child?"

"*Manuel, señor.*"

"The blind man?"

"*Sí señor,* he has lost his sight."

Estefan Ancona, as proprietor of an estate, enjoying many *peons,* or Indian slaves, held in light esteem the life of an Indian; but his own life had been certainly saved by the warning brought him by the boy, and he could not do less than listen.

"Where is your father, child?"

"On the cliff, in the *casita.*"

"Can we reach it except by going down the trail? It would be folly to walk into the fording-place which they are watching."

"*Sí, señor;* but the horse cannot go; there is a narrow path through the rocks; it comes out behind the *casita.* But hasten, *señor,* I pray you."

The pitiful face, lighted by its great, entreating eyes, looked up with such appeal that the rider could not resist.

"*Bien,* little one; one such favor as you have done me requires a re-quital; here Santos [to his *mozo,* who had just arrived], hold my horse; give me my carbine; wait here till I come. Now, *amigito,* onward!"

Bernalito led the way across the rugged barren, holding tight the revolver Señor Ancona had given him to carry, his limbs trembling, his heart heavy with fear. They reached the brink of the cañon and listened, — no sound. They entered a rift in the broad platform of rock, and descended toward the *casita,* — the little hut on the ledge.

"Have a care, *señor,* it is only a little way. Hark! Is not that *padrecito,* calling? Yes! it is; he is in trouble, in pain. Hasten, oh, hasten!"

The bandits had reached the *casita,* and had found the Indian sitting there motionless. The noise of their approach awoke him from his attitude of despair, and he cried joyfully, "Bernalito! At last!"

Chatto laughed fiercely: "No, old man; no Bernalito comes to you to-night. It is Chatto, — your friend Chatto. Did you ever hear of him? He has come to end your troubles."

Stupefied from disappointment, his victim did not answer.

Chatto stood by, maliciously noting his despair. "Speak, old man," he said.

"I care not for life, it is well if you end it; but my Bernalito, — have you done harm to him?"

"To him? Not yet: but I will, doubt you not!"

"And avert it I cannot! Father in heaven, care for my Bernalito!"

"That's enough. Come, are you ready?" The aged Indian made no reply, but clasped his hands, and raised his sightless eyes to the sky. His had been a joyless life; the end could come none too quickly. Chatto grew impatient; he was ill-satisfied with such submission, for he delighted in groans and cries, and struggles.

He seized the blind man by the hair, and turned toward the brink of the precipice; but at this instant a slight noise arrested his attention. Turning to the crevice whence it came, he saw the gleam of steel, and his quick apprehension at once grasped the situation. Loosing his hold, he darted behind a ledge, and a puff of smoke from the crevice warned him of the danger of delay. The report of Don Estefan's carbine had hardly died away ere the bandit was half-way down the cliff, and the *hacendado* himself knew that it was useless to follow him.

Aroused by the noise, the blind man groped about for some familiar object; he heard a well-known voice: "*Padrecito mio*, art thou alive?" And Bernalito pillowed the aged head on his shoulder and burst into sobs and tears.

"Bernalito, and hast thou returned? I waited long. my son; I was weary. I fancy that I must leave thee — and to whom? I could die happily did I know some one would care for Bernalito."

Don Estefan came forward then and took one of the wrinkled hands in his. "Manuel," he said, "I am here. Your boy saved my life; I will care for him and for you."

Bernalito looked up, brushing back his tears.

"And the *Médico, señor*, — the great doctor of Cordova?"

"He shall see your father to-morrow, or as soon as we can find him."

Thus was Bernalito's prayer to be answered. In the morning, as the first beams of the joyous sun struck the cliff, they wended their way down the cañon and went together to the *hacienda* near Cordova.

When *el Señor* had concluded, we all applauded, of course; for whatever the merits of his story, he had shown himself to be *muy simpático*, as the Spaniards say, or very sympathetic. Then we turned our attention to the country through which we were passing, and its history; for some of the most interesting episodes of the conquest of Granada occurred right here. The first act in the final drama played

LOUNGERS.

here by the Moors was, as we have said, the taking of Zahara by the Moorish king, in 1481. Then the Spaniards retaliated. In February, 1482, Rodrigo Ponce de Leon, Marquis of Cadiz, fell upon the lonely Moorish town of Alhama and captured it, holding it until succored by Ferdinand, against great odds. After that there was no rest for either Moor or Christian in Andalusia. One party or the other was raiding the populous towns or ravishing the fertile fields. Finally, after years of preparation, King Ferdinand himself came down. He

THE BANKS OF THE GUADALQUIVIR.

attempted to capture the city of Loxa, which lay right in sight from the railroad an hour or two after we had passed Antequera. The Spanish army was repulsed, but some years later succeeded in taking it, after terrible slaughter. It was in 1490 that the final preparations were made for the capture of Granada, the last stronghold of the Moors. Three or four years previously nearly all the towns around the great *vega* (or plain) of Granada had been taken, one by one. The name Granada is said to mean a pomegranate. Said King Ferdinand: "I will pluck out the seeds from this pomegranate, one by one, and then take the fruit itself." And so he did. He captured all the outposts, such as Illora and Moclin, and in April, 1491, sat down before the city of Granada with his army of fifty thousand horse and foot. In less than a year from that time Granada had capitulated, and the ancient capital passed out of Moorish possession forever.

The fall of Granada is said to have been hastened by the rivalry of two tribes, or factions, among the Moors themselves. Those of the tribe of the Abencerrages were the most noble and humane, and the most favorably disposed toward the Spaniards. It is said they were descended from the ancient kings of Arabia. The fierce African Zegris were their rivals, many of them descended from kings of Morocco, and they were bloodthirsty in the extreme, sparing no captives, and hating the Spaniards intensely. In Granada, the Moors had dwelt for two hundred and fifty years, until expelled by the armies of Ferdinand, in 1492. It was the last capital of the last Moorish kingdom in Spain, — their last hold in Europe. And toward this ancient capital, as the darkness of night fell about us, we sped across the *vega*, sleepy and tired.

CHAPTER XIII.

HANKS to our Spanish friends, we were not obliged to go to a hotel when we arrived at Granada, but obtained rooms in a quaint old house above the town, and near the walls of the Alhambra. Andalusia, the *Tierra de María Santíssima* (the "Land of the Most Holy Virgin"), comprises eight great provinces in the southern part of Spain, — Seville, Granada, Malaga, Cadiz, Cordova, Jaen, Huelva, and Almeria, — with over three millions population. In this territory are the finest cities of Spain, and the grandest cathedrals. We cannot more than allude to many of them; for, besides those of Andalusia, there are many others of great interest; such as Barcelona, on the northeast coast, with its magnificent harbor, its fine buildings, and memorials of the terrible Inquisition. A great exposition was held there this year (1888), to which all parts of Spain had contributed, and where all the people were represented. South of that lies Tarragona, likewise an ancient city, now famous for its wines; and still farther south, Valencia, the centre of a famous agricultural district, and a great hunting-ground in certain seasons. North of Valencia are the ruins of Murviedro, the ancient Roman city of Saguntum, whose inhabitants once perished in a terrible siege. But we are going to describe only Granada, and end our journey at the Moorish palace of the Alhambra.

TOMB OF FERDINAND AND ISABELLA IN THE CATHEDRAL OF GRANADA.

Granada, as we have already remarked, is said to have derived its name from the Moorish name for a pomegranate, as it stands on four hills, divided like a pomegranate. It is built on the edge of a great plain, fertile and highly cultivated, called the Vega, and runs around the bases and up the sides of two hills. One of these hills is crowned by the Alhambra, and the other by the Albaicin,—anciently the Moorish city. Between them flows the beautiful river Darro, which cleaves the city in two, and joins the Xenil on the southern side of Alhambra hill.

The principal street of Granada is called the Vivarambla, and used to run along the banks of the Darro, but now partially covers it, as the stream is covered over for a long distance. The quaintest street of Granada is the Zacatin, once the old market-place of the Moors, where they sold fine silks and jewels, manufactured by themselves. The finest building, of course, is the great cathedral, which covers the site of the Moorish mosque, and contains many rich articles of ecclesiastical furniture. Attached to this cathedral is the royal chapel, where lie buried Ferdinand and Isabella, those sovereigns of Spain under whom the Moors were expelled, and the voyages made whereby America was discovered. Their tombs are of the finest sculptured alabaster, and surmounted by the chiselled effigies of the king and queen. Beneath them is a vault containing four leaden coffins, enclosing their remains and those of their daughter Joanna and her husband, Philip. In an adjoining room are shown several relics of Ferdinand and Isabella, — his sword, and her sceptre and illuminated prayer-book. For Granada these royal personages considered the brightest jewel in their kingdom, and commanded that they should be brought here to be buried, wherever they might die. Their wish was fulfilled; and there they lie to-day, in marble effigy, as they have lain now nearly four hundred years, in the city they captured from the Moors. But it is not our purpose to spend further space in describing Granada, when its people are so peculiar and exceedingly interesting.

Though we stayed in Granada nearly a month, our spare hours, of course, were devoted to the Alhambra, and to excursions to various points of the Vega made interesting by their historical associations. The gypsy quarters above the River Darro frequently attracted us. There these peculiarly degenerate people, the Zincali, or Gypsies, dwell in caves hollowed out of the rocky hillside. They are dirty, dishonest, and inclined to mob every stranger who may seem afraid of them. How they live no one knows; but they are persistent beggars, and gain a great deal in this way, and by "telling fortunes." Their rude dances and wild songs may be heard at every fair and bull-fight (outside the ring), and they are the worst horse-thieves and jockeys in the world.

It took us a long while to get accustomed to Spanish ways, but after we did, we had little trouble. Perhaps their postal arrangements are the most curious to a stranger. To illustrate the extent of our credulity and implicit confidence in the perfection of postal regulations, it is enough to state the manner in which a letter is consigned to the mails in this land of Cervantes and Quixote. In the first place, you have no direct communication at all with those most concerned in the transportation of the mails. You have no disputes with the postmaster, as, for instance, who shall "lick" the stamps, or who shall pay the postage, for you don't see that official. The government guards against possible defalcation by depriving the officials of the privilege of selling the stamps. When you wish to buy stamps, you must go to the tobacco-shop. Government not only manufactures and sells cigars and cigarettes, — probably the vilest in the world, — but allows the tobacconist to sell postage-stamps, the authorized depositories for both being under the same roof.

The tobacconist is generally a lady, — at least she is a female, — and as you enter the shop with *buenas tardes* or *buenos dias*, she responds with elegance, and when you leave tells you to "Go with God," that being the literal rendering of *Vaya con Dios, caballero.*

FOUNTAIN IN THE ALHAMBRA.

After your letter is weighed, you affix the stamps and seek the letter-box. There is only one in the city, and that is supposed to lurk somewhere behind or beneath the yawning mouth of a lion, carved in stone or cast in iron, in the wall of the *Correo*. Having thrust your letter between the lion's jaws, and having heard it drop with a thud somewhere behind the wall, you then consider your duty done, and the subsequent responsibility rests with somebody you never saw and never heard of.

Of tobacco, a government monopoly, there are divers kinds, but no kind so poor, so wretchedly prepared, so altogether villanous, as that sold in Spain. As to whether or no we speak from experience, we are not going to commit ourselves; but enough is it to watch its effect upon the consumers of the weed. A certain acquaintance of ours who affects a great sympathy for the departed Moors because, we suspect, they *are* departed, and who hates the Spaniards for perhaps exactly opposite reasons, thinks he sees in this universal and inveterate consumption of vile tobacco a means of extirpation of the race now dominant in Spain. He assumes, first, that the tobacco furnished by government is a slow but sure poison; secondly, that nearly every male Spaniard is a consumer of this poisonous product; thirdly, that the Spaniard will soon succumb to the combination. In other words, the nation is slowly smoking itself to death, — the male majority of it. Its only salvation, in his opinion, lies in the fact that most of the women and the children are non-consumers. This whimsical opinion may have a little weight, and we give it for what it is worth.

But the Alhambra? Yes, patience yet a little; we will now visit it. The rivers Darro and Xenil are divided by a great hill called *Cerro del Sol* (or Hill of the Sun), and on the plateau where this hill overlooks Granada the Alhambra is built. A space of several acres is enclosed by a broken line of fortifications composed of walls and high towers. On the Xenil side rises the oldest towers of them all, the *Torres Vermejas* (or Vermilion Towers), said to be of Roman, perhaps even of Phœnician foundation. Opposite these towers, on another spur of the hill, is the Terre de la Vela, with strong fortifications, where the Christian banner of the Spanish conquerors was first displayed after the conquest in January, 1492. Here also is the Moorish bell which tolls throughout the nights during the

GATE OF JUSTICE, ALHAMBRA.

seasons of cultivation, regulating the irrigating of the Vega in some mysterious way that we could not understand. Just below it is the Tower of Justice, erected in the year 1348, a tower forty-seven feet wide and sixty-two high, with a high, arched doorway, the Gate of Justice, having a carven hand in its keystone, and inscriptions in praise of God. On the inside arch, and on another inner gate called Puerta del Vino, a key is carved, and Arabic tradition has it that

GENERAL VIEW OF THE ALHAMBRA.

when the hand outside shall reach down and grasp the key within, then Moslem Moorish power shall be restored in Spain; and it is not likely that it ever will be sooner. Inside this gateway, with its winding way, the khalif sat in Moorish times to give justice to his subjects.

Between the Vermilion Towers and the Gate of Justice is a deep valley filled with lofty elms, through which lead avenues, — one up the hill to the beautiful summer palace of the Moors called the Generaliffe, and others to either side. On the central one, above, two hotels are built, — the Washington Irving and the *Siete Suelos* (or Seven Vaults). Rapid streams run down the hill, fountains play in the *glorietas*, and nightingales sing sweetly here by day as well as by night. Climbing the hill through one of the lateral avenues, entering the Gate of Justice and passing beyond, you reach the *Plaza de los Algibes* (or Square of the Cisterns), so called because of vast subterranean cisterns beneath it where water is stored for use in the city below, and is carried thither by means of donkeys, and great jars on men's shoulders. Opposite this is a great circular building called the Palace of Charles V., because erected by that monarch, though never finished. It is an intrusion here, and should not have been allowed. The Alhambra, in Moorish times, is said to have been capable of containing twenty thousand people within its limits. It is a collection of great courts (or *patios*), about which are corridors, with tanks of water or fountains in their centres, and of towers at intervals, containing beautifully decorated halls. Enter with us now the first real court of the Alhambra, — the Arab palace built by successive Moorish kings. Its towers and walls overhang the Darro, and from their loopholes and windows most beautiful views are given the observer. Exteriorly these walls are plain and severe, and give no hint of the gorgeous rooms within. The first court we enter is called *La Berkah* (or of the Tank), because of a great fish-pond in its centre one hundred and twenty-four feet long and twenty-seven wide.

On two sides are beautiful corridors. and at one end rises the great tower of Comares, containing the celebrated Hall of the Ambassadors. This was the great reception-room of the sultans, and is even to-day most gorgeously decorated in color and in stucco adornment. Looking out of its windows, we can see right below us the river Darro, and opposite, the Albaicin and the rock-dwellings of the gypsies.

The most famous court here is the central Patio of the Lions, which was constructed in the year 1377. It is one hundred and twenty-six feet long, seventy-three wide, and twenty-two high, and its corridors and pavilions contain one hundred and twenty-eight slender marble columns. From two ends a marvellously beautiful porch or pavilion projects, with alabaster columns and lace-like stucco-work. In its centre is the celebrated fountain which has given it its name, — a great twelve-sided basin ten feet in diameter and two deep, upon the backs of twelve uncouth creatures which somewhat resemble lions. A tradition states that the children of the Moorish king Aben Hasen were all beheaded here on the edge of this fountain, — all except Boabdil, who alone deserved this fate, and who lived to ruin his kingdom. Two other courts open into this; one is called the *Abencerrages* (or that of the Royal Guard), because here were murdered all the members of a royal guard, and their blood-stains are still pointed out. This hall, as well as the one opposite (that of the Two Sisters), has a lofty, domed ceiling, composed of five thousand pieces of reed and plaster, and so wonderfully wrought and painted as to seem like a bit of heaven's dome itself brought down to earth. Across one end the Lions' Court is the Hall of Justice (*Sala del Tribunal*), seventy-five feet long and sixteen wide, with alcoves that once were occupied by divans; and it has most beautiful mosaics and iridescent tiles. Here, tradition states, the Moorish khalifs held court. Here Isabella once received in state. In the Hall of the Two Sisters and in various alcoves are latticed windows, through which the sultanas and princesses peeped, seeing, yet unseen, behind their jealously-guarded *jalousies*. Opening out of this great hall is a lovely little room looking into an orange garden with central fountain ; and this is known as the *Mirador of Lindaraja* (or the Boudoir of the Sultana), and is wonderfully rich in mosaics, tiles, and arabesques, and has a roof composed of bits of colored glass. Deep down beneath these halls and corridors are the extensive subterranean fountains, lighted only from above, through perforations in their roofs. Here are the alcoves where the Moors reclined after their baths, while their musicians discoursed delightful music in a gallery above. Through the perforated floor, at intervals, wafts of incense came up and lulled their senses into balmy sleep.

These are only the principal rooms, corridors, and courts; for there are many others, — more than we have space to describe. The Alhambra was indeed a dwelling fit for kings, and we do not wonder that the Moors declared that heaven and earth approached nearest together here. Many traditions are related of these palaces ; one of them states that the first king who built supplied himself with needed gold by the arts of the magician, and another kept an old man in a case, who gave him gold in exchange for his soul. Some of the best of these may be found in Washington Irving's delightful work on the Alhambra, but many others have never been translated out of the Spanish. We are pretty certain that the Alhambra was founded by King Ibn-al-Ahmar about the year 1248. so that some of it is over six hundred and forty years old, while others have been added by successive kings.

There is one pretty tradition we will relate, and this pertains to one of the towers outside, in the line of fortifications, and called the Tower of the Princesses. It seems that, some five hundred years ago, one of the Moorish kings found himself possessed of three beautiful daughters, and in order to keep them from running away, he shut them up in this great tower. He made it attractive as heart could wish, but yet they languished — for freedom, and perhaps for love. Now, it chanced that one of the king's captains brought to the Alhambra, one day, several Spanish prisoners, and shut them up in another tower, some three hundred feet away from the tower of the princesses. Of course, the natural result followed, as the captives (three of them, at least) were all good-looking, young, and unmarried, and they began making love to the Moorish princesses. That was just the sort of thing the princesses were pining for ; and the upshot of it was that they let themselves down from their windows, one dark night, and then all ran off together. And the two towers may be seen to-day, — the Tower of the Princesses and the Tower of the Captives, standing in the same places they occupied then, five hundred years ago.

Well, what more can we add ? We wandered for a month through the Alhambra, Granada, and over the Vega. We became acquainted with places and people, and so in love with them that we wanted to stay another month, at least. This could not be ; so we left Granada, and shortly after took our separate ways, — the Judge to return to France, the Professor and Historian to pursue their explorations into Africa; for we, having got a taste of Moorish ways. and a glimpse of Moorish architecture, in Andalusia, determined to cross over to Algiers, and thence on to Morocco and the region of the Great Desert. Thus it came about that our hunting-trip to Florida resulted in a voyage to the West Indies, the West Indies led up to Mexico, Mexico to Spain, and Spain to Algiers and the North Coast of Africa. Standing, as it were, at the portal to the Dark Continent, we will say *adios* (good-by) to our kind and gentle readers.